THE HAPPY ANT-HEAP

By the same author

Fiction

THE DAY OF THE FOX
THE VOLCANOES ABOVE US
THE TENTH YEAR OF THE SHIP
FLIGHT FROM A DARK EQUATOR
THE SICILIAN SPECIALIST
A SUITABLE CASE FOR CORRUPTION
MARCH OF THE LONG SHADOWS

Non-fiction

A DRAGON APPARENT
GOLDEN EARTH
THE CHANGING SKY
THE HONOURED SOCIETY
NAPLES '44
VOICES OF THE OLD SEA
JACKDAW CAKE
THE MISSIONARIES
TO RUN ACROSS THE SEA
A GODDESS IN THE STONES
AN EMPIRE IN THE EAST
THE WORLD, THE WORLD

NORMAN LEWIS

THE HAPPY ANT-HEAP

and Other Pieces

JONATHAN CAPE
LONDON

'God Bless the Squire' and 'Love at All Costs' were first published in *Granta*; 'Boris Giuliano', 'The Snakes of Cocullo', 'The Happy Ant-Heap', 'Where the Mafia Brings Peace' and 'Back to the Stone Age' in the *Independent* Magazine; 'A Goddess Round Every Corner' in *Departures*; 'Looking Down the Wells' in *Condé Nast Traveller*; 'Namek's Smoked Ancestor' in *GQ* Magazine; and 'Guatemala Revisited' in *Punch*.

Published by Jonathan Cape 1998

2 4 6 8 10 9 7 5 3 1

First published in Great Britain in 1998 by Jonathan Cape
Random House, 20 Vauxhall Bridge Road, London SW1V 2SA

Random House Australia (Pty) Limited
20 Alfred Street, Milsons Point, Sydney,
New South Wales 2061, Australia

Random House New Zealand Limited
18 Poland Road, Glenfield,
Auckland 10, New Zealand

Random House South Africa (Pty) Limited
Endulini, 5A Jubilee Road, Parktown 2193, South Africa

Random House UK Limited Reg. No. 954009

A CIP catalogue record for this book
is available from the British Library

ISBN 0-224-05171-7

Papers used by Random House UK Limited are natural,
recyclable products made from wood grown in sustainable forests.
The manufacturing processes conform to the environmental
regulations of the country of origin.

Typeset by Deltatype Ltd, Birkenhead, Merseyside

Printed and bound in Great Britain by
Mackays of Chatham Plc

CONTENTS

GOD BLESS THE SQUIRE

FORTY HILL WAS once the northernmost place from which people might commute to London. It was on the borders of Enfield Chase, a landscape covered with ancient oaks, many of them hollow, cleared, in the far past, of human habitation by terrible kings, and designed for hunting stags. The land and its hamlets were owned and ruled by Colonel Sir Henry Ferryman Bowles, a sporadically benevolent tyrant who would not have been out of place in Tsarist Russia. Further sharers in this rural emptiness were the Meux brewery dynasty and Field Marshal French, commander of the British Expeditionary Force during the First World War. He retired here in advance of the great slaughter on the Somme, having publicly admitted that this was a war he did not understand, and that could only be won by trebling the number of cavalry engaged up to that date.

From the age of five I attended Forty Hill Church School. Studies began every day with half an hour's catechism. 'Braithwaite,' the headmaster, Mr Eastaugh, would bark at a boy, 'what is it our daily duty to perform?' And Braithwaite would rattle out the first of a succession of dispirited responses: 'Sir, we must do our duty in that station of life into which it has pleased God to call us.'

It was here that many of us confronted the class issue for the first time when the Eastaughs' nephew began school, and pupils were instructed by Mrs Eastaugh that he was to be referred to not as plain Thomas but as Master Thomas. The same distinction was conferred upon a young member of the Bowles family, the feudal landlords of the area. A dubious state of health prevented him being sent over to the selective prep school, and he was delivered to us in Sir Henry Ferryman Bowles's Lanchester, a prestigious car of the day that appeared to have neither bonnet nor engine and was driven by a chauffeur in a green uniform. Master William, from the day he was settled smilingly at his desk in a small space respectfully cleared in the classroom, was evidently not quite right in the head. We took to him, for it was clear that he shared the democracy of the insane. Idiocy had released him from normal tensions. He made happy inarticulate noises, giggled endlessly and splashed ink on the walls. Mr Eastaugh was lavish in the use of the cane, especially in the case of young girls; Master William, however, was not only above corporal punishment, but strenuously objected to others being subjected to it. Thus all of us benefited from his presence and were sad when he finally left us.

Isolation in relatively empty country, crossed with byroads going nowhere in particular, had never quite released the village from the previous century. An early photograph of it could have been of Russia in about 1913, with small houses of all shapes scattered about a ragged little prairie remaining deep in mud or dust according to the season. Livings in Forty Hill, too, had always been scraped, and this, added to its cut-off location, made the place a sort of museum of outworn social attitudes that could only be remedied by more freedom of movement and more cash in pockets.

Sir Henry owned everything down to the last rut in the road and the last tiny cabin perched over the cesspit at the bottom of narrow village gardens. The exception to odd hutments and bedraggled terrace houses were a few better dwellings inspired by a grand tour Sir Henry had undertaken, which had included the Italian Riviera. He had liked the architectural style of San Remo and had several houses built to remind him of it. The result disappointed him as the development was in an area where a number of deep gravel pits had been dug. All the new houses had been given glamorous Italian names. 'What does *Buonavista* mean?' Sir Henry asked to be reminded. But the promised view was of the eroded slopes of a chasm with a stagnant pond at its bottom, and the new buildings were sold off cheaply to anyone indifferent to their surroundings.

The village possessed a few small shops giving tick to impoverished customers, a bookmaker, an alcoholic doctor, and two pubs in which sorrows were drowned in sourish ale at fourpence a pint. It had an immense fake-Gothic church and a canon of St Paul's with a voice like Pavarotti's for a vicar, who with his glowing pink cheeks and magnificent beard looked like an embittered Father Christmas. On Sunday mornings he preached powerful sermons to a congregation of country folk gathered in the three rows of pews behind the front row occupied by Sir Henry, his family and house guests. Attendance otherwise was slight. For the evening service the normal congregation was five elderly ladies. The villagers had lost their faith.

Three-quarters of the inhabitants of Forty Hill were members of the working class, which itself contained subdivisions of the most complex kind. Most able-bodied men of the previous generation had worked for the squire or his relations; there had been some advantages and many drawbacks in this. Six social divisions existed among the estate workers. Those at the top carried out delicate manoeuvrings with plants in greenhouses, kept themselves clean in doing so and demonstrated more acquired skills than muscular power. Sheer strength was ill-rewarded, and at the bottom of the social pyramid were those who went out, whatever the weather, to plough Sir Henry's furrows.

Now, with the building of factories in the Lea Valley, half Sir Henry's labour force had deserted him, got on their bicycles and pedalled away down to Brimsdown where the implacable machines awaited them. They worked for 'good' money, among the voiceless chatter of machinery from which there was no escape until the end of the day. Sir Henry's esteem for his employees could never have compared with his affection for a well-trained working dog; nevertheless, esteem was conveyed in a word, a glance, a nod – even occasional stuttered syllables of praise – and Brimsdown offered none of these rewards. Moreover, estate workers passing through a door in an enormously high wall on their way home at the end of the day carried with them a trace of the atmosphere of protection and privilege in which they had worked.

Sir Henry paid little but showed no signs of shedding the courtesies of the past, never failing to ask after a grandmother's health or remember the name of a child. Brimsdown was unconcerned with such things.

One native of Forty Hill stood apart from the rest. This was Jessop, butler at Myddelton House, home of Sir Henry's brother, the famous botanist A. E. Bowles. Jessop, a bachelor with a house in the caste-ridden Goat Lane, had completed a course at a training school for domestic staff, where he had been urged to limit his utterances to five words appropriate to the subject, and to refrain from smiling in public. Although he had little to say and was rarely to be seen, his influence was great. People who came to him for advice were given five words that always proved useful, after which he turned away with a brief 'good day'. It was believed that both Sir Henry and his brother took his advice on village matters. Only Jessop, armed with respect, had triumphed over the class system in Forty Hill.

In the case of my own family, class divisions remained an enigma never fully understood. My parents, both from South Wales, now found themselves among people they could only study and seek to emulate with, at best, partial success. The social complexities of Forty Hill were wholly foreign to rural Wales. Carmarthen divided its citizenry into three classes based upon wealth, language and the forms of religious observance. At the bottom of Welsh society the country people, mostly smallholders, spoke and sometimes only understood Welsh, and worshipped in Welsh Baptist chapels where not a word of English was heard. Above them came the townspeople of modest means, usually English Baptists who had ceased to speak Welsh but belonged to chapels where sermons preached passionately in English were acclaimed by loud cries of assent. The third category was made up of rich and successful members of the Church of England who were calmer in their approach to the Almighty – most of them could have passed for the real English across the border some sixty miles to the east. At this level of Carmarthen society it was demeaning to be heard uttering a word of Welsh, and some parents, such as my grandfather, even urged teachers to punish children overheard speaking the old language among themselves in school.

A problem in Carmarthen was the extremely limited choice of surnames. There were Morgans, Reeces, Davises, Thomases and Joneses galore, and for this reason the acquisition of double-barrelled names was an intelligent solution. Thus something was done about a town with a population of 10,000 of which 400 were Thomases, and I often wondered whether this useful device had been invented in Carmarthen and then spread to the rest of the country.

My grandfather appeared on his birth certificate as plain David Lewis, but having made a killing on the salvaged cargo of tea from a ship sunk in Swansea harbour, became thereafter David Warren Lewis, and all the members of our extended family, except my father, gladly followed him in this bold change of style.

My father, having started promisingly enough in London as an analytical chemist, had then taken employment with a drug company where he found himself involved in the production of Beecham's Pills. Later he moved into a ramshackle shop in Enfield Town, where, having come to believe that all medicines were poisons, he devoted himself to the sale of homeopathic remedies that depended almost entirely upon faith for their effect.

He decided to settle in Forty Hill because houses in these dishevelled surroundings were cheaper than elsewhere. Our home was semi-detached with no more than a partial view of a pit. The name originally given it by Sir Henry was *Isola Bella*. This, although there were no other numbered houses in the vicinity, my father hastily changed to number three.

Relations between Sir Henry and the village were going through a bad patch at this time. Although it was three years since the end of the First World War, field sports had not fully recovered, to some extent through the loss of gamekeepers and the time taken to train new recruits. As a result the pheasants left in peace for so many years had become so plentiful that they were to be seen everywhere, not only at the roadside but in the gardens. Cases were reported to Sir Henry of his tenants making meals of these errant birds, and his fury was said to have been terrible to behold. 'My God,' he screamed, 'they couldn't even shoot them decently. They actually used traps.' So stung was he by their ingratitude that he was reported to have threatened offenders with eviction.

These incidents coincided with charges in the popular press that, despite the sacrifices of their elders, the new generation was lacking in ideals. An example of this was reported in the *Enfield Gazette and Observer*, deploring the conduct of a number of teenagers in the local cinema, the Queen's Hall. This was a run-down fleapit charging a minuscule admission for a programme of outdated and often damaged films. The cinema had been urged to foil its patrons' habit of making a dash for the exit immediately before the ending of the last film to avoid having to stand to attention for the National Anthem.

This was to be done by locking the exit door five minutes before the show ended. The cinema complied, but having heard that they were locked in, the audience joined in a vocal accompaniment of the pianist with a ribald version of the anthem inspired, it was said, by the public image of Edward VII:

God save our old tom-cat,
Feed him on bread and fat,
Long live our cat.

My only encounter with Sir Henry had happened at an earlier period, at the age of about eleven. His reputation for accessibility encouraged me to trudge up the long drive to his mansion at the top of the hill in the hope of gaining his consent through any intermediary who would talk to me to go bird-nesting on the estate.

I banged on the door, which was opened by his butler, but behind him, to my surprise, came Sir Henry himself, who waved the butler away and took over. Before this I had only seen him at a distance, and now at close quarters I realised he was small and unimpressive compared with, for example, the imposing Jessop, who by my standards put all other local males in the shade. He asked me what I wanted; I told him, and he began his reply, stopped suddenly then broke into a stammer, blinked, then after a silence the words poured out. Where Jessop would have dealt with me in five words, Sir Henry needed fifty. Behind him the room sparkled like an Aladdin's cave, a tall, willowy girl twirled as if in the arms of a partner to the music of a gramophone, there were flowers everywhere, and for the first time I drew into my nostrils the spiced aroma of wealth.

What surprised me most was that this man who ruled our lives should appear to be pleased to see me. In between the stammer he smiled affably. Bird-nesting was permitted and not only that, he said, but he would have liked to come with me to show me the best places for nests, but unhappily he had to address a meeting of the Primrose League that afternoon. 'Never mind,' he said. 'Come back and see me next week, but make it the morning when there's less going on.'

When I got back home, my mother asked me if I'd seen any of his lady friends, and I told her about the girl dancing by herself. 'That's the one who reads poetry to him,' she said.

In later years I heard more about these 'relations', as the females who surrounded him were known. They came and went. There was the poetry reader, a games mistress who kept him fit, a young nurse who told somebody in a pub that all she did was inspect his urine. He kept several aristocratic ladies living in cottages on the estate with nothing whatever to do with their time but 'visit'. They were the bugbear of Goat Lane, where the women had too many children and too many household tasks to have time to entertain these uninvited guests with empty chatter. But these visits were a matter of routine, and every house in the village would be visited several times a week; there was no way of escaping these intrusions.

The harassed wives and mothers of Goat Lane had little left to defend but their pride. Callers at the house for any purpose were expected to knock at the front door once or twice, and if there were no response to go away. Sir Henry's relations avoided this protocol by going straight through the tiny garden, usually littered with rubbish, to the back entrance. A soft tapping on the kitchen window would draw reluctant attention to the smiling face, and the woman of the house would realise that her poverty was on display. Unavoidably the kitchen door would be opened upon washtub smells, a grubby overall, soap-sodden hands, tired eyes and straggling hair. The visitor would be seated resentfully and offered weak, milky tea, while her victim settled with what grace she could muster to inane chit-chat, punctuated with the yowlings of her children.

It was an election that furnished the only instance of open opposition to Sir Henry's reign. As Conservative candidate he would normally be returned unopposed, but once, and to everyone's surprise, a most unlikely challenger came on the scene – a Liberal who happened also to be a pleasant young woman. Next a Liberal poster appeared in a Goat Lane window, put up by an old nightwatchman in one of the factories, thought of as weak in the head. At the weekend Sir Henry's steward called on him to drop a hint that, as in the case of the phesant-trappers, his tenancy of a tied cottage might be at risk. Any estate worker would have caved in on the spot, but with this the first glimmerings of proletarian solidarity were evident, for although no more Liberal posters went up, several Conservative ones were taken down. For all that, Sir Henry won in a landslide.

Life in the country had undergone much dislocation during the war and had continued to suffer from shortages of every kind for so long after its end, but was beginning to pick up again. Agricultural produce, still in short supply, fetched satisfactory prices. Farmers admitted to not doing so badly after all and could afford small increases in wages. The big houses were taking on staff, and girls brought up in the poverty-stricken democracy of the Lane now became domestics dressed in fashionably old-style uniforms, working fourteen-hour days and learning from butlers such as Jessop how to return short toneless utterances to orders received, 'Will that be all, madam? Shall I clear away now?' A better class of car was back on the roads with the appearance of a beribboned Bentley from Brimsdown snuffling softly through the dust of the Lane on its way to a wedding.

At this time of recovery and renewal the first shoot on a pre-war scale took place over Sir Henry's land. It was organised in a precisely planned fashion by Sir Henry and landowning friends, all of them military men and accustomed to dealing with bodies of men in warlike situations. First came the long front line of beaters followed by twenty-four guns on a half-mile front. Birds with no experience of such a disturbance scuffled aimlessly through the trees and fell an easy prey to the lady pickers-up with their dogs and the small steel hammers known as priests with which remnants of life would be deftly extinguished.

So successful was this pheasant holocaust that it was judged to have been almost worth waiting for. Champagne kept for such an event flowed in abundance, and the euphoria generated gave birth to the idea that an equivalent event – a fair of some sort – should be organised for the village. It was a project enthusiastically backed by Sir Henry himself, who despite his tyrannical outbursts remained a boy at heart and was noted for a passion for fairs. Until precluded by the disciplines of war, these had been held in his grounds on every possible excuse.

It was the brilliant idea of Canon Carr-Smith that Empire Day – 24 May – should be chosen for this popular occasion on which a good time for all could be linked to pride in the possession of an empire which, leaving out the emptiness of the seas, now covered one-sixth of the globe. By this time I was in my last term at Enfield Grammar School, where the art mistress had produced a huge map in which these overseas territories stood out in brilliant scarlet among the extremely dull colours of those left in the possession of foreigners. This formed the background to the assembly-hall stage from which local dignitaries addressed us on imperial topics on the eve of the great day.

The fair held at Forty Hill was to outclass all previous entertainments of the kind. On the night before, the village had been full of the iron noises of tractor engines crashing through the potholes, and by mid-morning on the twenty-fourth a great, garish encampment, so alien in this rustic setting, covered the summit of the hill and spread aggressively through the grey-green monochrome of hedgerows and fields. It was peopled by gypsies with fierce, handsome faces, flashing eyes and shrieking voices from whom the locals drew nervously away. At the entrance each child was presented with a Union Jack, but after a few perfunctory waves, these were tossed into the bushes.

Blocking access to swings, roundabouts, coconut shies, hoopla stalls, fortune-tellers and gypsy boxers who could defeat local challengers with ease was a large tent bearing over its entrance the sign PEOPLES OF THE EMPIRE. Into this the villagers were firmly directed and here they were faced by a row of dark-complexioned men lined up on a platform, all in colourful – sometimes astonishing – garments, most baring their teeth in efforts to smile. Placards at their feet denoted their place of origin. Some of them had feathers stuck to bare chests, others wore tasselled loincloths, turbans or coolie straw hats, and carried clubs and spears. (In fact they were Lascars recruited from Bombay and shipped over to work on the London Docks, where they had been tracked down by Sir Henry's agent and fitted out by a theatrical costumier to play their part.) The children giggled nervously at the sight, and a few of the younger ones showed signs of alarm. We were told to clap and we did, and the 'people of the Empire' bowed gracefully or waved.

Beyond this bottleneck the fair was in vigorous action, and those who finally escaped joined others who had bypassed imperialistic propaganda by better knowledge of the geography of the grounds. Life in Goat Lane was a matter of leaden repetition, and the whole village, apart from the bedridden and a sprinkling of misanthropists, was here for that tiny taste of excess that would encourage them to tackle survival with a new burst of energy.

The fair organs ground out their music, and the steam engines blew their exultant whistles. Despite the blatant cheating that went on, some of the cleverer villagers, whooping their triumph, won on the games. At first, inexplicably, the latest in roundabouts brought specially from its place of manufacture was not in use, with access to its grinning, wide-eyed horses debarred by a rope. A dozen of the elderly estate workers wearing ceremonial collars and ties lingered in its vicinity, and shortly the lights came on, a preliminary gurgling started in the organ pipes, a woman's face appeared in the window of the little ticket office, the rope was removed and it was clear that action was about to begin. Two men approached carrying an armchair, which they placed with its back to the roundabout, and with that Sir Henry came on the scene and took his seat in the chair. He was wearing his decorations and a grey bowler with a strong curve in its brim. By this time the old men had formed a line and now they moved forward one at a time to take Sir Henry's right hand in a gentle squeeze and mutter a greeting suited to the moment. Sir Henry smiled and stuttered his thanks, then turned away to climb the steps of the roundabout, hoist himself up on a horse and begin his solitary ride. The crowd applauded, Sir Henry raised his hat, the roundabout began its rotation, while the organ wheezed into 'Alexander's Ragtime Band', still the anthem of moments such as this.

Such entertainments had to be paid for, although prices, subsidised by Sir Henry, were low. No charge was made for teas, and there was a bun fight for the children, also free. This could have been the last survivor anywhere of a traditional revel providing for the young a joyful escape from plain food and much amusement for those who looked on.

The bun fight at Forty Hill was held in the stable yard, where three trestle-tables had been lined up for children momentarily released from disciplines that would imprison them again at the end of the day. Bun fight was an accurate description of what was to happen. The buns brought up from the bakery in large wicker baskets were tipped out on the table tops, and the children scrambled and pretended to fight for them. Sir

Henry and several landowning friends invited to be present found these scuffles picturesque and were ready with their cameras. I remembered a previous occasion when the then prime minister, Stanley Baldwin, who had been at Harrow with Sir Henry, had turned up to applaud the maintenance of a custom so deeply rooted in our history. This year the feeling among the organisers was that, due to the dispirited quality of the times, the thing was calming down. The children fought each other on the table tops as tradition demanded, and cheeks were scratched and hair pulled, but it was a tame affair, and no blood flowed.

The women of the Primrose League who had inspired such antipathy among the housewives of Goat Lane were present. They made neat piles of the remnants of demolished buns before clearing them away and smilingly righted mugs that had been knocked over, refilling them with lemonade made from crystals of citric acid.

Jesus said of the poor 'they are always with you'. In Forty Hill it was the rich who were rarely out of sight.

1996

A MESS OF A BATTLE

THE SIGNING OF the armistice that put Italy out of the war was announced from the Municipality of Naples at 6.30 p.m. on 8 September 1943 to a large but remarkably inert crowd assembled in expectation of the news. The ringing of hand-bells on occasions of public rejoicing had been ordered by the fascist state. This was left to a minor functionary, who did so in a lackadaisical fashion, and an attempt at spontaneous dancing in a nearby side-street soon petered out. Maresciallo de Lucca of the *carabinieri* listened to the announcement and to the dispirited murmurings of the crowd and recorded their reactions in his notes in shorthand of a kind used by the police, which in this case took the form of four letters: PVDP, translatable as 'No acclamation. Cries of give us bread.' He returned to his office in the Piazza Dante, and in a matter of minutes a telephone call from the *carabinieri* colonel commanding the area came through. He ordered de Lucca to leave immediately for the area south of Salerno, remove the files from a list of police stations and return with them to Naples. In addition he was to visit the shrine of San Gennaro at Santa Maria della Fossa, take possession of the sacred relics comprising several finger bones of the martyr and arrange for them to be placed in safe keeping in Naples.

De Lucca found the order baffling; nevertheless, he dashed off in his car, emptied the police stations listed of all records of their transactions, then sped on to Santa Maria, where he arrived on the scene too late, for the caretaker had deserted his post and thieves had already decamped with the precious relics. Turning back for Naples, he heard a warning come through on his car radio of a total curfew on all forms of travel. Remembering old friends who were staying in their holiday cottage on the beach at Paestum, he went there to ask for a bed, and spent the last hours of the day in pleasant company, playing cards and discussing theories of perpetual motion, in which all were interested. They were late to bed, and at dawn de Lucca got up, left the others asleep and went down to the beach a few hundred yards away, in the hope of being able to collect shellfish among the half-submerged rocks. Despite the brilliance of the morning, his eye was caught by what seemed a low sash of mist extending from one end of the horizon to the other. For the time of year the mist was exceptionally dense, giving an impression almost of solidity, and studying it more intently it seemed that indistinct objects were forming in it. Within minutes these vague shapes took on edge and solidity, until they become identifiable as ships.

A month later, while on an official visit to the *carabinieri* headquarters in Naples, I met de Lucca, an engaging man who described this experience, which he had never quite recovered from, in person. 'I stopped trying to count all the ships,' he said. 'They were spread out for miles. I thought: what can they be doing? There's nothing for them here.' Presently lights twinkled among this grey confusion. This de Lucca interpreted as naval gunfire, and turning his attention as if by instinct to the profile of mountains over the beach, he saw a house plucked from a distant village like a tooth from an old jaw.

He went back and awakened his friends. 'I think we're being invaded,' he told them.

At 5.30 a.m. on the day when de Lucca had watched the ships take shape in the mist, ten British Intelligence Corps members, including myself, were studying the details of the distant Italian coast from one of them. We had sailed from Algeria in the *Duchess of Bedford*, carrying the entire HQ staff of the American Fifth Army, and had dropped anchor some ten minutes by landing craft from Paestum beach. Our ignorance of what awaited us there matched de Lucca's as to the reason for our coming. We had been told of the armistice, but otherwise all was hazard and conjecture. Supposedly the Italians were out of the war, but where were the Germans? Were they still present in southern Italy – and if so, in what strength? A lecture delivered by the fleet's Chief Intelligence Officer the previous evening had ended with the startling admission, 'We know virtually nothing.' This confession did nothing to inspire confidence in the outcome of what awaited us. In addition it was known that the Fifth Army was composed largely of troops who had not seen action and was led by generals whose first taste of battle this was to be. The majority of the officers had taken comfort in a belief that the landing would be carried out without opposition, but this illusion was hastily jettisoned when the first landing craft to approach the shore came under heavy fire. For those of us still on the ship, waiting to climb into a boat, Paestum lit by the first rays of the rising sun appeared as a scene from antiquity: three Greek temples sparkled distantly among pinewoods backed by a low crenellation of mountains. Over these a slender column of smoke arose from a village that had attracted speculative fire from the ships.

Twelve hours passed before we were finally put ashore among American soldiers by the thousand, wandering without direction in aimless, bewildered groups. There was an unnatural silence about these men drifting through the shadows, broken rarely by the low murmur of voices. An MP jeep on the lookout for wanderers or men who had lost themselves crawled softly by, its tyres crunching on the sand. A single shot spread sharp echoes and startled movement. It was a scene imprinted with fear.

For us it was an occasion not wholly free from risk. We had been warned on the ship that our British uniforms might seem strange and even alarming to young soldiers exposed to foreign surroundings for the first time, and we had been advised to have ourselves kitted out by the quartermaster as soon as we were ashore. There was the matter of the password, too. Here and there sentries had been posted and one suddenly sprang out of a bush, rifle aimed, to demand a password, of which we knew nothing. It came close to being a lucky escape, and at this point the essential problem seemed to be to eliminate the hazards of our first night on Italian soil. We therefore chose a dense wood in the vicinity, burrowed deep into the underbrush and almost instantly fell asleep. Some time later I was awakened by movements through the bushes. Listening, I picked up a low mutter of voices, among which I could clearly distinguish German words, forming the opinion in a drowsily relaxed fashion that these could only belong to the enemy, on the lookout, as we had been, for a place to pass an undisturbed night. Soon the voices died away, and I slept again.

Early next morning we reported for duty at what was pointed out to us as the Fifty Army HQ's staff tent. We were carrying papers addressed to the Staff Officer (Intelligence) describing the urgency and importance of our mission, but we discovered that neither this officer nor any other senior member of the HQ staff was present, and after diplomatic questions put to the captain who saw us, we learned that the whole staff from General Mark Clark down were still aboard the *Ancona*, 'where there was more space'. According to our briefing in Oran, we were to instruct senior officers, who in many cases would be seeing action for the first time, in the revelance and importance of security. Our suggestion was that we might be taken out to the *Ancona* to contact the Intelligence Officer there without delay. The captain's reception of this request reflected both harassment and boredom. 'We're under pressure here, as you can see,' he said. 'You want to be of use right now, maybe you should give a hand unloading supplies.'

We looked down upon the long, thin trail of humanity wandering like ants through the sand dunes down to the water to pick up their burdens and return. Sergeant-Major Dashwood explained the urgency with which 312 Field Security Section had been brought up, at the insistence of General Clark himself, from the depths of Algeria to provide safeguards essential to the opening of the Italian campaign, but listening to him the captain's expression changed to hardly concealed hostility. 'In that case,' he said, 'you are free to come and go as you please, and to occupy yourselves as you think fit.' It was the last we saw of him, and we accepted the fact that we were now on our own. Nevertheless, perhaps out of habit we were unable to stifle an interest in what was going on. The Fifth Army HQ troops fixed up field kitchens, knocked together rudimentary sleeping quarters for officers and other ranks, dug latrines and unloaded boats. A mammoth pile of typewriters and filing cabinets began to accumulate, but no weaponry, artillery, ack-ack guns, mortars or even rolls of barbed wire were reaching us from a marine horizon glutted with uncountable ships. But above all – and far more alarmingly – where were the tanks?

Despite the limitless chaos, D-Day at Paestum had gone as well as expected, but two miles or so to the south on what was called Blue Beach the situation was less promising. A landing in the face of machine-gun and mortar fire had produced a number of casualties and a master-sergeant to whom I chatted was taking a number of corpses back to one of the ships. They had been laid out in the bottom of a boat, their faces covered with clean napkins, arms fully extended and thumbs along trouser creases, as if in preparation for an inspection by Death. This boat, like all the others in the vicinity, had come in laden with office equipment, which now formed high piles all along the waterfront. Once again, the boat had brought with it no weapons.

The German presence in the area was now guaranteed, although there was still no precise information as to where they would be dug in, awaiting the Fifth Army's advertised attack. As there was nothing better to occupy me, I took one of the section's motorcycles and rode some three miles along the beach in a northerly direction, through fine coastal scenery, past tamarisks growing under ancient Mediterranean oaks, with a single glimpse of a water-buffalo of the race imported by the Greeks, knee-deep in a swamp.

I stopped briefly to inspect the empty seaside house which, from my subsequent conversation with de Lucca, was clearly the one occupied by his friends on the night of our invasion, and then again at the point where the Sele River runs into the sea. Shortly before my arrival a squad of engineers had blown up a bridge a hundred yards away carrying both the north–south road and railway line over the river; at the moment I drew up they were finishing off boxes of K-rations and taking snapshots of each other. I asked the engineers why they had blown up the bridge and was told that it was to hold up any kraut advance. My friend the master-sergeant had given me a rough map of the bridgehead which included this area. 'But it's the British sector,' I said. 'What would the krauts be doing here?'

'Search me,' was the reply.

I showed one of the engineers the master-sergeant's map. 'Going north as far as you can see is British,' I said. 'All the way to Salerno.'

'I wasn't told that. I guess the guy who gave me the order didn't know, either. So maybe there's no one here. Maybe it's empty. I guess the British were waiting for us to do something about it and we were waiting for them.'

'Let's hope the enemy hasn't heard anything about this,' I said.

On the second day, in the hope of making our stay more comfortable, we moved into one of the small farmhouses abandoned in the vicinity. The symbols of panic seemed more poignant in these humble surroundings. The first huge crashing salvoes from the fleet had demolished the carefully calculated order of this shrine of domesticity. A single window had been blown out, a child snatched from its cot had dropped a doll, and a pair of crushed spectacles lay on the floor. Country people with lives organised to defend this low level of prosperity were known in these parts as *famiglie di una vacca* – one-cow families – and in this case, sure enough, the sole cow had been sacrificed to the invaders' hunger for fresh meat, and it lay within sight of the back door, a haunch hacked away.

We returned to camp in time for the first alarm call to reluctant battle as a German plane broke like a shining white splinter from behind the cliff and curved, in a manoeuvre appearing calm, leisurely and even beautiful, to drop a single bomb among the ships. Through our master-sergeant friend we learned that a landing strip had already been cut to enable our fighters to fly in from Sicily and take on the intruders. Unfortunately the first of these, a Spitfire, fell victim to friendly fire while attempting to land later that day.

With the vision of the German FW 190 skimming over the cliff-top above us, all illusions entertained about this battle were at an end. Wild talk of Naples in four days and Rome by the beginning of the month was silenced and in its place defeatism began to spread. Two or three old soldiers, who had seen action in North Africa and found themselves among these raw beginners from Kansas and Wisconsin, realised that any Allied attack when launched would meet with the resistance of one of the best-armed, most sophisticated and tenacious forces in the West. There were even pessimists ready to suggest that far from the predicted military walkover, the Fifth Army might find itself involved in a defensive battle. These doubts strengthened later in the day when attacks by a single plane were replaced by those carried out by a five-plane squadron arriving overhead punctually at intervals of one and a half hours.

The Germans' obvious takeover of an airfield left no doubt that an immediate counter-attack was likely. No attempt had been made by the Americans to secure the heights overlooking the beach-head, and in the absence of this precaution it seemed more than likely that the enemy would do just that. Altavilla, some six miles away, dominated this area and as a precautionary measure, since no Germans were there, General Clark called for a naval bombardment which left this mountain village in ruins, with substantial loss of life. This was opposed by his own staff, and General Walker later wrote, 'I did not see how the destruction of buildings and killing of civilians in Altavilla was going to help our situation.'

Infantry units were now called upon to begin limited advances into the encircling hills, but since at this stage no armoured or artillery support was available, some clashes with the 16th Panzer Division's Mark IV tanks were catastrophic. Blue Beach to the south now came under enemy artillery fire, and the attempt to land the first of the Fifth Army's tanks here was frustrated. There was a day's delay before the tanks could be brought ashore on Red Beach, within sight of our farmhouse at Albanella.

The mediocre performance of the first two days ashore was responsible for the growth of something like a military inferiority complex. The FW 190s came and went at will, and any hopes of discouraging them faded after a second and third Spitfire from Sicily succumbed to friendly fire. Rumours were an important part of the Intelligence Corps' stock-in-trade and an ideal place to collect them was in the evening chow-line, through which they flowed like a ceaseless current. Pessimism was general, but it was of an informed character and bolstered by fact. General Clark, still out of sight on the *Ancona*, was fighting his first battle command, which was considered a bad start for those who served under him. The soldiers knew that Clark was at loggerheads with his subordinate generals, Dawlish and Walker, and that was a bad thing, too. Among the many rumours, most damaging was the one that Clark was already contemplating withdrawal and would approach the British Navy for their support. Attempting to trace the source of such rumours, it became evident that high-ranking officers on the *Ancona* talked with extraordinary freedom in the presence of the staff who served them in the mess. The Commander-in-Chief, a showman with a propensity for bullying his inferiors in public, was deeply unpopular with the troops. The sergeants expressing their views freely in the chow-line were of the opinion that Clark had done whatever he could to postpone 'Operation Avalanche' until Montgomery's Eighth Army, coming up from Sicily, was in the vicinity, and preferred even now to defer an advance.

Minor probes into hilly country by infantry unprotected by tanks and without air-cover came to nothing when they ran into opposition, although Altavilla, devastated by the naval guns, was found to be empty. Clark and his staff now left the *Ancona* in search of ample accommodation for his headquarters ashore. It was inevitable that he should be shown the grandiose abandoned mansion known as the Villa Rossa, a folly full of statuary and old masters – inevitable, too, that he should have decided to move in. Thus, after the huge effort to bring a mountain of HQ equipment ashore and stack it, protected from the weather in a safe position, it now had to be humped by office staff and off-duty soldiers up to the villa, which was only accessible by narrow tracks.

In the old days aristocratic visitors to the Villa Rossa from Rome would have been dropped off at Albanella, within walking distance of our farmhouse. At the time of our arrival the village had been abandoned, with the exception of a shop selling sour white wine and an aphrodisiac cheese famous throughout southern Italy, made from the milk of local buffaloes mixed, it was said, with dried and ground-up flies.

The woman who ran the shop was outside whitewashing her doorstep and seven Sherman tanks were lined up across the road in the shade of a hedge. This was the morning of Day Four, and these were the tanks sent to the wrong beach on Day Three and which, escorted by destroyers, had finally been brought ashore at the point originally intended. The day was fine and the atmosphere calm, although in the distance there was a sound of thumping, like a fist on a heavy door. Having finished her task, the woman went inside and came out with several tiny glasses of wine, which she presented to the soldiers about to carry out the first armoured attack. The soldiers threw away their cigarettes, gulped down their wine, waved to the onlookers and climbed into the tanks. Moments later the engines started and the tanks rumbled away. At the end of the street they turned into the mountain road, and one of the bystanders said, 'They are going to take Altavilla from the Germans.' The ruins of the village had now been occupied by enemy troops.

After about an hour had passed, two of the tanks returned, driven in a way that suggested they were almost out of control. One charged past, climbed a bank and crashed through a hedge into a field. The other slewed right round and stopped, and the crew came through the door to fall weeping into each other's arms. Thus ended, with the loss of five tanks, the Allied attack on Altavilla, and with this the curtain rose at last on the long-awaited battle.

In the evening chow-line back in Paestum the details of the sad happenings of that day were common knowledge. The sound of artillery fire was now clearly audible; the Luftwaffe, punctual as ever, was more brazen in its attacks, and some young Texans had formed a circle to pray in loud voices.

Moving onto the offensive, two American columns set out to ford the Sele River, possibly in the hope of blocking any enemy advance down the river valley to the coast. The attempt was frustrated by the 16th Panzer Division, and the attackers withdrew in disorder. Thus, whenever the Germans decided the time was ripe to push down to the sea, there was little but the fire of the gathering battleships to stop them.

In view of the failure of our mission and in the hope of securing our release from what had become an absurd predicament, four members of our section set out on their motorbikes for Salerno, using a track along the edge of the beach, and faced with the certainty that sooner or later they would have to pass through the German lines. While the rest of us remained in reverent occupation of the farmhouse, we decided as a matter of prudency, as the sounds of combat between the anti-tank unit and German Panzers advancing from the north came closer, to dig a slit trench between the house and the sea. Should the worst happen, our intention was to take to the water and swim along the coast until we reached an area where it looked safe to come ashore.

This crisis apart, this was a pleasant place and the time was passed chatting to displaced persons and Italian soldiers who had hastily demobilised themselves and were on their way home, and to the crew of a British 3.7 anti-aircraft gun, who had been due to land at Salerno but found themselves put ashore at Paestum. The sergeant was bewildered but phlegmatic. 'We're supposed to defend a gap,' he said. 'Is this it?' 'Yes,' I told him, 'but there's not much you can do. It's ten miles wide.' 'I see,' he said. 'It doesn't make sense. So what am I supposed to fire at?' 'Tanks,' I told him, 'coming down the river.' 'This gun is designed to fire upwards,' he said. 'If it has to fire at tanks, we have to work on it to drop the angle. Feel like giving a hand?' This we did and after an hour or two the gun pointed straight ahead. 'You don't seem to be too worried about this?' I asked him. 'I'm not,' he said. 'I was at Dunkirk. After Dunkirk nothing worries you.'

While this conversation had been going on three lost American infantrymen had wandered into sight. Somewhere in the Sele Corridor they had surrendered to a German tank. There was no room to take them aboard, so the tank had run over their weapons and let them go. That evening, in the last of the line-ups for chow before this procedure was abandoned, I was told by Americans of the same 45th Division to which these strays belonged that their orders were to take no prisoners, but to use the butts of their rifles to beat to death those who tried to surrender. At the time I rejected this as an exceedingly twisted form of boasting, but later, when I was in the field hospital with malaria, this story was repeated by several of the wounded and there was no option other than to accept it as a possible, if shocking, truth.

Day Four was one of assorted adventures and alarms. From dawn on, enemy planes were constantly overhead, weaving and twisting through the grey bruises left by the naval ack-ack shell bursts in the lemon sky. The artillery fire, previously no more than a soft thunderous rumble through the hills, was now recognisable as such with faintly audible blasts and concussions. Strain showed in the wary expressions of those who listened. The soldiers' small-talk had dried up and their faces were thin, perhaps as a result of the absence of cooked food, which had now been replaced by packet K-rations containing ham, cheese, biscuits and sweets, all but the last being frequently thrown away.

The removal of the Fifth Army's headquarters from the *Ancona* to the Villa Rossa was now complete, with most of the furniture and the senior officers comfortably installed, when the alarm was raised that spearheads of an armoured German column were within three miles. With this, a hasty evacuation of the villa began and General Clark moved into a mobile caravan. He was reported to have pressed US Admiral Hewitt to agree to re-embarkation, but his plea had been rejected by both Hewitt and the British Navy, because it was too reminiscent of Dunkirk, and also on the score of the thousands of tons of supplies that would have to be abandoned.

At the villa a 'last-stand' defence-line was organised, and MPs began a forceful mobilisation of all members of the villa's staff considered capable of firing a gun. These included office clerks, maintenance personnel, electricians and bakers, and – outstandingly – members of a military band who had ill-advisedly volunteered to entertain guests at the headquarters' formal opening. The defenders were given a choice of guns or spades. Heroic military rituals such as this, we were told, had been inherited from the American Civil War.

Having completed the enforced recruitment of the headquarters' staff, the MPs dashed about in jeeps in search of other slackers and inevitably we fell into the net. They arrived while we were enjoying the last of the afternoon sun behind a sand dune. Light carbines were shoved into our hands and we were ordered to be ready to join the nearest resistance group, should the feared emergency arise. The news of General Clark was that he had ordered a tank landing-craft to stand by in case he and key members of his staff needed to escape to British General McCleary's headquarters in Salerno.

Shortly after nightfall, and in bright moonlight, the battleship *Warspite* arrived offshore and began bombarding the German tanks in the Sele Corridor. Shells from its fifteen-inch guns passed overhead in clusters of fiery points, and as they struck home the trench shuddered, as if struck by the waves of a distant earthquake. At one point a major arms dump blew up and a great pulsating halo spread, twinkling with sparks and throwing out sensitive feelers of fire, across a half-mile of sky. At some time in the early hours three tanks came into sight a mile away at the edge of the beach, moved towards us, then turned back.

At 4 a.m., notwithstanding our conviction that we had been forgotten, an armoured car arrived to lead us on our motorcycles to an olive grove two miles to the south. This short journey involved us in the only serious danger we had encountered in the battle. Obliged to skirt a last-stand line, we were fired at by the defenders, who believed that they were being infiltrated by the enemy. There were blood-curdling screams from those hit by the bullets.

In the olive grove we joined a rabble of shocked, demoralised and even weeping soldiery. Our hope was to find just one senior officer who could perhaps calm them and convince them that they would neither be captured nor killed. But there were no officers here. Demoralised too, they had abandoned their men in a *sauve qui peut* panic and taken refuge on the ships, and it was late in the morning of the next day before they began to reappear. While these depressing happenings had been taking place, 500 paratroopers of the American 509th Parachute Regiment had been flown in to save the battle by creating a diversion in the enemy's rear, being dropped up to twenty-five miles off target and a number on the roofs of buildings in Avellino from which, unable to disentangle themselves from their gear, they fell to their deaths.

Salerno was advertised and planned as one of the decisive battles of the Second World War, linked with the huge prestige of the return of the Allied armies to Europe. But with the collapse of the Italians, the Germans had no interest in remaining in southern Italy and, having fought no more than a series of delaying actions at Salerno, withdrew in good order. It was a withdrawal no more than accelerated by the news of the approach of Montgomery's Eighth Army from Sicily. Of this battle General Alexander wrote in his *War Diary*, 'The Germans may claim with some justification to have won, if not a victory, at least an important success over us.'

Thus, for 312 Field Security Section of the British Army, a mess of a battle had come to an end. We gathered up such belongings as had survived the confusion, mounted our motorcycles and rode off into the devastated landscape, making for the vast urban enigma of Naples, where our next year was to be spent.

1997

THE PRIVATE SECRETARY

THE SECRET PROPOSALS for the destiny of a liberated Austria at the end of the last war were no more impractical, even absurd, than any such army schemes. They were under discussion at Security Headquarters at Castellammare, southern Italy, and were listened to against a background of soft guffaws by section members with some experience of operations of the kind. Experts neutered by the unreality of a non-combatant war were sent out from London to speak of the many war criminals who had taken refuge in this basically pacific country, from which, at the moment of defeat, they would slip away across the Alps to Italy *en route* for South America. A plan devised to baffle them was explained. It involved the encirclement of the whole country by hundreds of miles of unscaleable and impenetrable electrified fencing, linking radar-equipped strongpoints at twenty-mile intervals. Behind this fence the whole Austrian population, both military and civilian, would be confined, prior to investigation in the equivalent of a vast concentration camp, while Allied forces dealt with the expected pockets of armed resistance with firmness and precision.

Nothing in the history of warfare approached the

ingenuity and the scale of this planned undertaking, yet when the talking was at an end, and we were finally despatched to the Italian frontier with Austria, our mood was one of profound scepticism. It was characteristic of this adventure that the Intelligence Corps sergeant with whom I had joined forces, a PhD in Hellenic studies, should be fluent in Greek of the time of Pericles, but spoke no German. We arrived at the Brenner Pass three days after the cessation of hostilities. According to the plan, this should have been firmly closed, with a mixture of thirty-odd million Germans and Austrians penned in behind the fences awaiting our arrival. The stunning fact was that the pass was wide open and we squeezed our lorry into the roadside as a grey avalanche of humanity slid down through the valleys towards us. The fugitives were on foot or being carried in every conceivable conveyance from farm-carts with peasants wedged in among their cattle to a circus steam-engine towing a truckful of performers, a few even still dressed for the ring, with a caged bear on a trolley. Many soldiers who had torn the distinguishing marks from their uniforms were mixed in with non-combatants of every kind and all ages. No one would ever know how many responsible for war crimes had been able to hide themselves away in this desperate snail's-pace exodus into the neutrality of Italy.

Some hours later, radiator spouting steam, we reached the top of the pass ready for the view of the first of the strongpoints, the electrified fence and the searchlights that would turn the Alpine night into day. Of these nothing was to be seen, and even the post with its notice proclaiming the frontier's existence had been dismantled and thrown to the roadside. Soon, with the frontier hardly two hours behind, we discovered in Austria an extraordinary normality. The war had never come as far as this and, with the first of the Russians still 200 miles away, Austria remained a fragment of the dismantled empire of the Hapsburgs. Country people free of wartime controls came and went as they had always done. It was a journey into the past, full of picture-postcard Tyrolean scenes: farmers in *Lederhosen* with wooden pitchforks, yoked oxen, and gigantic mountain dogs bounding to snap at our wheels.

On the second day we reached our destination, the small Alpine town of Engelsdorf. Here there were houses painted with flowers and angels in flight, and churches with enormously high steeples and clocks with little hammer-armed figures revolving to music as they struck out the hours. Carts replacing the cars that had vanished were drawn by oxen with splendidly carved horns. Women wearing billowing skirts and bonnets kept the streets clean and scraped the ox-droppings into neat piles. We stopped for a girl herding geese, and later saw another shoeing a horse. From this small town all the men had been carried off to the war. Stopping, we listened to the silence, broken only by the tinkling of the ox-bells, which was to continue through day and night. Engelsdorf smelt of milk.

No hotels were open so we moved into a *Gasthaus* run by a Frau Pauli, possessor of the fairest skin, the blondest hair and, as a result of her endless labours, the hardest muscles of them all. She was assisted in her never-ending tasks by two girls, also blonde, beautiful and muscular. Sometimes they broke off from whatever they were doing to watch with bereaved eyes as a squad of newly arrived young British soldiers marched by.

Asked what had happened to husbands or lovers, the answer was, 'Sir, the house-painter [Adolf Hitler] carried them away to Russland. We do not think we shall see them again.' Work, perhaps, saved them from repining, and for the abandoned women of Engelsdorf work was unending.

Two hundred yards from the *Gasthaus* at the end of the street three wonderfully polished cannons pointed down the open road to a checkpoint a couple of miles away on the boundary of the Russian zone of occupation. Germans still in uniforms rumpled from sleeping rough wandered aimlessly along the roads outside the town and we first ignored them, then came close to forgetting their presence. There were rumours of last-ditch stands being planned by Nazis who had not surrendered, and following investigations we concluded that they might be correct. Back in the imperial days, the milk barons of Engelsdorf had built vast semi-castles in which to enjoy the views over the mountains, lying in folds at the back of the town, and there were reports that some were occupied – and would be defended – by regrouped SS formations when the time seemed ripe. We in fact discovered a vast, decaying mansion with the SS still in possession, and borrowed a half-company of infantry from the nearest Army HQ to deal with the crisis. What followed was something of an anti-climax, for having arranged for the surrounding of the supposed redoubt, my friends and I went in through the front door to find the SS occupants already lined up, as if on parade, in the principal room in readiness for the offer of their surrender.

The takeover by our troops of this corner of south-east Austria provided hardly more excitement than the routines of civilian life. We learned of the commanding general's concern that the hunt for war criminals had produced scanty results and that he had spoken of his hope that the presence of trained security personnel might remedy the situation. By chance our arrival coincided with the capture of our only big fish to date, a Gestapo chieftain called Heinrich Poldau, whose mistake it had been to stay quietly at home instead of mingling with the streams of displaced persons and ordinary soldiers who no longer attracted attention. The nature of Poldau's service committed him to a somewhat solitary existence and he had taken a small house out of town, where he had lived with an Austrian girl who had decamped as soon as the first reconnaissance car flying the Union Jack drove into Engelsdorf. Frau Pauli knew this girl, who had whispered to her of the Secretary's secret activities. Now our hostess rushed to tell us of the prize lying within our grasp and later that day we picked him up.

When I met him I realised that I had known almost exactly what to expect. This was a quiet man who concealed himself behind the façade of a small bourgeois life, a man who knew how to enter and leave a room without the occupants being aware of his presence. The house he had chosen to rent was a showpiece of domestic clutter. Trinkets of all kinds were pinned to the walls of his living room, and a pair of stuffed owls held a stuffed mouse apiece in their claws. There was a shelf full of decorative pipes, and a faded print of the Redeemer, who, apart from his oriental garments, could have been a middle-class Austrian of the last century. This assemblage of objects if anything strengthened an underlying sensation of emptiness.

Poldau was a neat man in one of those rough-surface woollen jackets popular whatever the weather in places where mountains are sometimes in view. His hands were well looked after. He wore a plain ring and a plain watch. I was most taken by his face, which reminded me of one of those serious portraits carved in stone in the porch of a Gothic cathedral, depicting more calculation and less religiosity than those of its neighbours. I explained why I was there and he listened intently, nodding his head at the end of each sentence. Finally I told him he was under arrest and he bowed slightly and said, 'At your service.' I gathered from his accent that his English was good. I took him back to the *Gasthaus* where the girl called Fruli came down dust-covered from mending the roof, to serve him an evening meal. He was exceptionally polite to her, but she dumped the food down, turned her head and flounced off. After the meal I accompanied Poldau to the town jail – a medieval building entered through a portcullis – signed the register and left him to the jailer who, as usual in such institutions, appeared more than a little mad. Poldau's only reaction to his caperings was the slightest trace of a smile.

Back in the *Gasthaus* I sent off a hasty note by dispatch rider to the Staff Officer (Intelligence) at Klagenfurt. 'Poldau, Heinrich, believed Gestapo, held under arrestable categories. PIR follows.'

There was a reply within the hour. 'Good luck. Ascertain urgent priority whether Poldau with *Einsatz Gruppen*, Poland and Russia.'

The problem next day was where best to talk to this man. The prison environment is the one least likely to foster relaxed and possibly revealing conversation.

Rough guidelines for dealing with such situations were offered in a leaflet passed out at Security Headquarters containing for me at the time the truly remarkable suggestion that the suspect under interrogation should be taken, if the surroundings were suitable, for a quiet walk. Bizarre as it sounded, it seemed in these circumstances not altogether a bad idea. As a precaution I borrowed a rifleman from the RA unit and then, collecting Poldau at the jail, told him we were going for a stroll in the country.

We drove up steeply into the foothills of the Glein Alps rising from the back of the town, and stopped for a last view of its pinnacles and golden roofs through the oaks spreading their foliage like a tinsel decoration in the summer light. I parked the car and told the soldier we were all going for a walk in the woods and he nodded, worked the bolt of his rifle and dropped a bullet into the breech. An extraordinary transformation took place in Poldau's manner and appearance. He breathed out, then laughed. 'Why is he afraid?' he asked. 'The war is over. No more war.'

'He's not the slightest bit afraid,' I told him. 'He has orders to carry out.'

Poldau laughed again, as I speculated on the change he had undergone. Now it was all over. The game was up. In some way he could now relax.

We set out on a narrow path through the woods, the soldier in the rear humming a monotonous tune.

'I have some questions to ask you,' I told him.

'Whatever you like,' he said. 'I think the time for secrets is at an end.'

'What is your rank in your organisation?'

'We do not speak of ranks. Only duties. I am a secretary.'

'Tell me how you were recruited.'

'That is simple. It was by accident. I was born in Görlitz near the Polish border, where most people spoke some Polish. When the talk of war began there was a call for Polish speakers. We were told only that the matter was confidential, having some connection with the police. It was of interest to me because the pay at the bank was very low, and because successful candidates would not be subject to military call-up.'

'So that was the Gestapo?'

'It was not a name we ever used. I was officially listed a member of the Statistics Bureau of the Security Police. After a few weeks' training I was sent to Poland.'

'Tell me something about your activities there.'

'Really it was no more exciting than the bank. It was office work as before, but I was sometimes employed to question Poles who were unable to speak German. With the end of the campaign I returned to records and statistics in Bremen. In the end I asked for an interview with the Chief Secretary and told him I was bored. He was sympathetic and said I could not be allowed to resign, but I might take six months' leave to join the army, after which I would return to the office.'

'So you got six months' leave from the Gestapo merely for asking? I find it hard to believe.'

'The Bureau was very flexible,' Poldau said – I thought with a touch of pride. 'I was encouraged by the Chief Secretary to take courses in army organisation and the Russian language,' he went on. 'After that my leave came through. I was under the minimum height for the Waffen SS, but the Chief organised things for me and I got in with the rank of *Standartenführer*, and was sent to the Eastern Front.'

'When you were in action in Russia were you a member of an *Einsatz Gruppe*?'

'Of course,' Poldau said. 'All soldiers with my qualifications were automatically directed into such groups. Let me explain that their task was to ensure nothing could hold up the speed of our army's advance. Large areas of enemy territory were surrounded by our pincer movements in a matter of days and many prisoners taken without a fight. Thus thousands of these were left behind. Our regular troops could not speak their language, and *Einsatz* groups took over.'

'And many starved?'

'They starved because an army moving at high speed can carry provisions only for its soldiers. In a single day we might take twenty thousand prisoners and be compelled to leave them behind. Camps had been designed to hold them, but they could not be made ready in time. When two hundred thousand prisoners were taken and brought to Stalag VIIIB, we found this to be no more than a square of ground with no buildings of any kind. This was inevitable, because the roads were blocked with snow.'

'Were you at Salsk?' I asked.

'I was at Salsk, where not only the Russians but we ourselves came close to starving. It was ten days before food reached us, and then there was little of it. The Russians ate the bodies of their comrades who died from sickness or starvation. At first there were struggles over dividing up human meat, but then we permitted only doctors and butchers among the prisoners to do this, and order was restored.'

The rifleman, eager to listen to such gory details, had come closer and I waved him back.

'How many died in all?'

'In Salsk there is no way of knowing, because in some cases only the bones were left.'

'I mean in all the camps.'

'Figures were never given. Five million? Ten million? Perhaps more. I could talk to Russians but never understand their mentality. In battle they laughed at death. When we attacked our orders were to kill all wounded Russians left lying on the ground, because otherwise they would drag themselves to their knees as soon as we had gone through and shoot us in the back.'

I was beginning at this point to question how much of this catalogue of horrors it was necessary to include in the report. A vague multitude of men had vanished from the earth as if through a monstrous conjuring trick. No more than a legend, eventually to be forgotten. The figures were guesswork. Those who had kept records had themselves been swept away, so there were to be no names on Russian memorials, no epitaphs to be inscribed. As García Lorca had written of a single brave man killed by a bull, 'a stinking silence settled down'.

We walked on and Poldau spoke eagerly, as solitary men sometimes do, of his childhood and background, and reverently of the skilful surgery of modern warfare as demonstrated in the blitzkrieg by which France had been overthrown in a matter of weeks, compared with those slogging years of trench warfare in the First World War. Only the snow had put an end to Germany's dream of carrying its eastern frontiers as far as the Urals. 'Not only Germany but Europe has been defeated,' he said, 'and Bolshevism remains intact.'

I returned him to prison, finished the report and took it to the Staff Officer (Intelligence), a classical scholar whose habit it was to slip admiring references to Caesar's campaigns into discussions of the military chaos of Austria. Major Stevens was a worrier also, distraught at that moment at the news that Russian Asiatic troops had broken into the town and were chasing all the women in sight. He ran through the report. 'My God,' he said. 'This man mustn't be allowed to slip through our fingers.'

'He won't. He comes into the arrestable categories. Pending further investigations, we can hold him as long as we like. But that's as far as it goes.'

'Even if he was involved in mass killings?'

'That has to be proved.'

'You say here he was at Salsk. Isn't that the camp where Russian Jewish prisoners were forcibly fed with excrement and drowned in urine?'

'Poldau denies that the Final Solution was ever employed in the *Stalags*. He admits the death total was high, but says that prisoners died of diseases, hunger and the cold.'

'What was this man doing in Engelsdorf?'

'He was sending back stories he'd made up about Austrian separatists so that they'd keep him here. He knew that Germany was finished and decided to lie low until it was all over. His plan was to stay here until things settled down, then change his identity and go home.'

'Could we use him?'

'In what way, sir?'

'It's been confirmed that war-criminal trials are to be

held. This man was there. He's seen it all. He would make a sensational witness. Perhaps he could be sounded out?'

'In a way that's already been done. I believe he would agree to anything we propose.'

'With some sort of inducement no doubt?'

'It might help.'

'There's little we could offer. All these people will have to be let go in the end. Might be able to speed up the process, that's all. Any question of financial inducements has to be ruled out.'

'Money doesn't interest him. He's an abstemious sort of man. Strangely infantile. He had a collection of toy railway engines and is fond of animals. He mentioned he'd carried a white rat as a mascot through the Russian campaign. It died through eating unsuitable food. He likes painting.'

'What does he paint?'

'Sea views.'

'Is he married?'

'No. He is too devoted to his mother, he told me, to marry. The worst thing for him about the Eastern Front was that her letters took up to three months to come through.'

'In a way none of this surprises me,' Stevens said.

'It didn't surprise me either, sir.'

'Any thoughts as to what might help to bind him to our purpose?'

'So far as I'm concerned, discussions are complete and as soon as they're ready, he'll be sent to one of the camps in Germany. They're opening one near Bremen, where his mother lives. If it could be arranged for her to visit him there, I'm sure he would show his appreciation in any way he could.'

'Well, I imagine we could do something about that,' Major Stevens said.

1997

MEMORIES OF AN INDULGENT BURMA

I AM PROBABLY one of the few persons to have been tipped by a taxi driver, instead of the normal reverse of this transaction being the case. It was a small matter, yet provided an unforgettable moment of illumination of a cultural and spiritual divide between the East, as represented by Burma, and the West. The driver, affectionately known locally as Oh-oh, charged reasonable sums for ferrying Burmese passengers in his canary-coloured taxi about the southern town of Moulmein, but offered his services free to foreigners deposited there for a day or two when the ship from Rangoon put into port. Most of these fares, Oh-oh had heard, were enjoying a temporary escape from the capital, where visits into the surrounding countryside were not permitted. Like so many of his countrymen he was constantly on the alert for an opportunity to acquire merit, and being kind to foreigners came under the heading of meritorious actions. When the *Menam* tied up, the yellow jeep would be seen waiting on the quay, with Oh-oh offering a free ride to the new arrivals to any part of the town, plus a visit to the pagoda at Mudon, a few miles away, if the road happened to be clear of insurgents.

At the end of such trips passengers received a small present in the form of an ornament cut from mother-of-pearl. In my case the gift was a superior-quality bird's nest. We had visited the caves where the earliest of the season's nests were being collected, and this was the first 'number one' nest of that day. It had probably been finished only the day before, and was therefore spotlessly clean – a tiny amber saucer constructed from secretions in glands located in the bird's head. The collector gained merit, too, by giving it away, and we shook hands and he congratulated me with a wide smile when Oh-oh passed it over.

Oh-oh now proposed that we should take breakfast – it was by this time midday – by joining a party given by a local family to celebrate the entry of their son into the Buddhist novitiate. We found ourselves in a large hall in which we joined about 200 people seated upon mats on a polished floor. Oh-oh assured me that our host had collected many of the guests at random off the streets. Girls dressed in old-style finery were going round distributing snacks of pickled tea-leaves, salted ginger and shredded prawns. Once again merit-gain was what mattered, and it was an occasion for the family to give a substantial portion of their possessions away. It might take them two years, Oh-oh thought, to settle the debts incurred by this entertainment.

It was Oh-oh who warned me, when I told him of my hope to travel in the interior of the country, that I should do something to modify the extreme pallor of my skin. 'They will not stare because they are polite,' he said, 'but the young people in the villages have never seen an Englishman before and they will believe you are Japanese. We are entertaining bad memories of these people.'

'What can I do about it?'

'You may make your face darker by keeping it as much as you can in the sun.'

I took this warning seriously, and after three days' exposure as suggested on the deck of the *Menam*, my skin was the colour of freshly cut mahogany, except for white circles left by the sunglasses round the eyes. This caused some amusement among the European passengers, but evoked the sympathetic concern of the Burmese, one of whom being the assistant purser, who confided in me his belief that I was the victim of witchcraft.

There was no outright prohibition on foreigners travelling in the interior of Burma at this time, six years after the conclusion of the Second World War, but those who arrived in Rangoon found that such were the obstacles encountered in their efforts to do so that they soon gave up. When I presented my letter of introduction to U. Thant, head of the Ministry of Information, he saw no reason why I should not go where I wished. Later he admitted that, this being his first experience of a request to travel in the country, he was not sure of the official procedure to be followed. Later still I was to be informed that the US Military Attaché had fared no better and that a team sent by *Life* magazine to do a picture reportage had left after two uninteresting weeks spent in the Strand Hotel, Rangoon.

The days slipped away while I was passed from office to office, handled always with wonderful courtesy, encouraged in my hopes and commiserated with upon my many frustrations. Escape was by the greatest of flukes. Someone told me that a certain powerful general was the only person who could do anything for me. I was admitted to his office to be received by a man overflowing with charm. My face was by this time covered in blisters, but whatever surprise he may have felt at this spectacle, nothing of it showed. The fluke consisted in his occupation at the moment of my arrival with the translation of a recently issued British military manual into Burmese, and the difficulties he had run into, for although he had been at Sandhurst, certain of the terms employed had since then been changed. 'Happen to know anything about this kind of thing?' he asked, and amazingly enough I did. One hour later I left his presence with the pass in my pocket that was open-sesame to any part of Burma. 'Damn interesting trip, I should imagine,' he said. 'Won't find it too comfortable, I think, but have a great time.'

The question was where and how to travel at a time when the Burmese army was at grips with five different brands of insurgents in the provinces, and the small town of Syriam, just across the river from Rangoon, was under attack by dacoits. The disruptions of war had left a gap of a dozen miles in the main line connecting Rangoon with the old capital, Mandalay, and steamers using the Irrawaddy to carry goods and passengers up-country were sometimes cannonaded. Travelling rough could still be undertaken on the lorries of traders generally supposed to have come to an arrangement with insurgent bands, but there was nowhere in the interior to stay, not even a single hotel, and the dak bungalows providing rough accommodation in the past were closed or had been destroyed.

Happily Mandalay could still be reached by plane, and two days later I landed there, to be met by Mr Tok Gale of the British Information Service, who told me that he had arranged for me to sleep in the projection room of the town's only cinema, and would do his best to find a seat for me on a lorry going north. I was astounded to hear that he lived in what was officially described as the town's dacoit zone, two miles away. Tok Gale instructed me in the protocol of travel by Burmese lorry. Drivers, he said, did not accept money, but it was in order to present them with small gifts, and he suggested that I should carry such items as key-rings and plastic combs. Postcards of the coronation of George VI were also eagerly collected and he had brought along a selection of these. 'You will be seated next to the driver,' he said. 'Please take trouble to compliment him on his driving skills whenever occasion arises.' There was a word of warning. 'Beware in conversation of disparaging dacoits. These persons may be respectably dressed and mingling unobserved with lawful passengers.'

The night of my arrival in Mandalay, while walking in the deserted main street, I was attacked by a pariah dog, which bit me calmly and quietly in the calf before strolling away. Fortunately the only place of business open was a bar, where I bought a bottle of Fire Tank Brand Mandalay Whisky to disinfect the wound. I increased my popularity on the next leg of the trip by sharing the remainder of this with such of my companions who were not subject to a religious fast. From this experience I learned the usefulness of religious fasts when rejecting unappetising food, such as the lizards in black sauce served in the north of Burma in roadside stalls.

The first stretch of the journey was to Myitkyina, where the road came to an end in the north, followed by a route virtually encircling the north-east, through Bhamó, Wanting – almost within sight of China – and Lashio, then weeks later back to Mandalay. At Bhamó, in jade country, you could pick up beautiful pieces of jade for next to nothing, and to my huge delight a circuit house for travelling officials (although there were none) was actually open, run by a butler straight out of the Victorian epoch, who addressed me as 'honoured sir', instantly provided tea with eggs lightly boiled, and later a bed with sheets.

A final adventure was protective custody, into which I was taken in the small town of Mu-Sé. Once again I slept contentedly, this time in a police station, and by day was accompanied by a heavily armed policemen, who was as much interested as I in wildlife and natural history, on pleasant country walks.

Thereafter all was plain sailing. Children had long since ceased to be alarmed by my ravaged features, and pariah dogs were no longer perturbed by an alien smell. At Bhamó again, I took the river steamer down the Irrawaddy to Mandalay – a pleasure-making excursion', as the man who sold the tickets described it, and he was absolutely right. For three days we chugged softly through delectable riverine scenes. We were entertained by a professional story-teller, musicians strummed on archaic instruments, and once in a while the girls put on old-fashioned costumes to perform a spirited dance. There was a single moment of drama that was more theatrical than alarming. Insurgents hidden in the dense underbrush at the water's edge fired a few shots. Those on deck took momentary refuge behind the bales of malodorous fish piled there. No one was hurt and by the time I arrived on the scene from below, our military escort, who had blasted away at nothing in particular, had put down their guns and gone back to their gambling.

Next day Tok Gale welcomed me back in Mandalay.

'No complications with journey, I am hoping? No bad effects from meeting with dog?'

'None at all. Everything went off perfectly. Couldn't have been better.'

'I am relieved. Well at least something will be done now about all those dogs on our streets.'

'So, you're actually getting rid of them then?'

'For a while, yes. Abbot U Thein San is taking all these animals into his pagoda compound for feeding and smarten-up. They will be released in a better frame of mind. It is belief that they will give no more trouble. In Mandalay we are used to seeing them. We should be regretful to miss their presence.'

'It's to be understood,' I said.

'So how are you planning return to Rangoon?' he asked.

'I'm taking the train.'

Tok Gale seemed doubtful about this. 'For train travel they are saying that things are worse than they were. Rangoon train never arrives at destination.'

'I've been hearing that, so I took the precaution of having a horoscope done at the stupa of King Pyu Sawhti.'

'Ah yes. This is famous monarch hatched from egg. And was result satisfactory?'

'Entirely so. The *ponggi* told me I was good for another thirty years.'

'Well, that is splendid omen,' Tok Gale said. 'So 6.15 to Rangoon is holding few terrors for you?'

'How can it after a horoscope like that?'

Tok Gale laughed and shook his head in mock reproach. 'Now I must tell you something, Mr Lewis. You are falling into our ways.'

1997

HOLD BACK THE CROWDS

EVEN BACK IN the early Fifties it was more interesting and usually more pleasant to travel in areas of Europe off the beaten track. In this respect Spain was outstanding, due largely to damaged communications in the aftermath of the Civil War. Many roads had been left unrepaired for a number of years, with the result that most Spaniards travelled only when obliged to. Foreigners, on the whole, still nervous of the Franco dictatorship and discouraged by rumours of food shortages, were staying away. For my first post-war visit I found the frontier between France and Spain still nominally closed. I had to take a French taxi to the frontier post, walk through the barrier, then hire a Spanish taxi to the first town across the border. Despite all that had happened I found Spain as charmingly unspoilt as it had ever been, and hiring a car I went in search of a seaside village in which to spend the summer.

I chose Farol on the Costa Brava and as it turned out spent three summer seasons there, studying and writing about the life of the people. Protected by an approach down something hardly better than a cart track, followed by steep gradients and hairpin bends, and a final patch of swamp crossed by a swaying bridge, the village was perfect from my point of view. A further slight drawback to the visitor was that a spare room in a house had to be found, although in a friendly and hospitable environment this offered no difficulty. Such were these small deterrents that in the first of three incomparable seasons of my stay, there were no other intruders from the outside world and in consequence I was able to enjoy life in surroundings that had hardly changed in the previous century or two.

Apart from the priest, a shopkeeper, and a Civil Guard, the people of Farol lived wholly by fishing, and even a young doctor possessing the legal minimum of qualifications for practising his profession put in an hour or two dickering with the nets with which he caught an occasional fish. There were neither rich nor poor, and even the charming old aristocrat who owned most of the land grew on it no more than a few meagre vegetables, and stole out at night to put down pots from which once in a while he recovered a lobster. Life here, although devoid of modern stress, provided an abundance of small pleasures. The fishermen back from the sea told tall stories and composed poetry in the single bar. On Saturday nights there was dancing to a wind-up phonograph in the tiny square. Fiestas were frequent, as well as outings to accepted beauty spots and local shrines. For financial reasons courtships were protracted and marriages entered into later in life than in the towns. Families with more than two children were rare. Above all, it seemed to me, the villagers lived in harmony. The fisherman's calling is the least boring of professions, for however meagre the daily return, hope of great catches to come is never extinguished. Fishing where large shoals are frequently involved calls continually for communal planning and action as opposed to individual effort. In Farol, a living constructed from the sea was devoid of any taint of bad blood.

I was late on the scene the next year, and by then the first of the tourists had arrived. They were two French girls who had found a room over the bar, but who soon moved on, although their brief presence left an extraordinary effect. The fishermen's wives who spent most of their day mending nets spread out on the beach had been much impressed by their clothes, and had copied them carefully. Within a matter of weeks, still busy with torn netting, they were clad in reasonable imitations of French fashions. These, although unsuitable to the background, attracted much admiration both in Farol and in other villages in the vicinity. The accommodation over the bar had been rented at rather above-average prices, thus giving the couple who ran the place the idea of adding to their establishment an annexe with two more rooms. As soon as this was completed it was occupied by more French tourists, and a developer attracted as if by magic to the scene put in plans for a three-storey hotel.

By year three a startling change had come about. All the main highways from the frontier were now resurfaced, the potholes in the local roads filled in, the swamp drained and the bridge put in order. The new hotel, 'modernistic' in design, dominated the mild contours of the old village like an army strongpoint and was full of English and French, and the foundations of two new hotels were already in place. Dances were arranged for the foreigners every night, and the young fishermen, having overcome their shyness, joined in. Most significant and even disturbing was the news that two or three had abandoned the sea to work as waiters in the hotel and a café that had opened, and in doing so made far more from tips than the most experienced fishermen on the boats.

I was shown the plans for the further development of Farol, which was to include a marina, a sea-front promenade, several restaurants, more hotels and a large car park. By the time all this was completed what had once been a tiny village would have become a town with suburbs. Someone mentioned that there had been emotional disturbances. Two local betrothals had come to nothing following fifteen-day romances with foreign holidaymakers, and one promising young fisherman had gone off, taking nothing but his guitar, and no more had been heard of him. The time had come, I decided, to move on.

In 1984, after an absence of thirty-four years, I returned to Farol on a visit suggested by a London newspaper. I had suspected that I should find it unrecognisable and this proved to be the case. What I drove into after formidable traffic delays was a *Costa* city stamped out as if by some industrial process. Part of the village's original charm lay in the straggling irregularities of its narrow streets. Now they had been blasted and bulldozed into a uniform width with buildings of a standard design. A one-way system corkscrewed its way down through a firmament of traffic lights to a point where I knew the sea lay somewhere ahead, but it was invisible behind hoardings. Moments later I was to find that most of the beach had become a car park, with long lines of cars and notices warning of the danger of theft. Back in the streets there were burger restaurants, amusement arcades and advertisements for go-kart racing, and a refulgent sign in English urged *Let's Go Play Cowboy Games*. Fishing was at an end, but fishermen who could not bring themselves wholly to abandon the sea had fitted glass bottoms to their boats and took tourists on trips 'to explore the beauties of the coral gardens'. (Both the coral and the huge shells with which the sea-bed had been littered were of Pacific origin.)

I ran to earth one of the old friends with whom I had gone tunny- and sardine-fishing so many years before. He seemed, strangely enough, to have been saddened by what should have been a tremendous stroke of luck. Shortly after my departure he had inherited a valueless scrap of land in the village's centre, on which his wife had kept chickens. Twenty years later he had sold this for several million pesetas, putting most of the cash into a scheme to convert a sluggish stream on the town's outskirts into a canal with gondolas in the Venetian style. The project had come to nothing, for no method had been found to stop the water seeping away.

'Do the girls still wear those Parisian dresses they used to put on to mend the nets?' I asked.

'No,' he said. 'They all work as laundresses or chambermaids these days. It wouldn't be suitable.'

'What about the poetry they used to recite in the bar?'

'If you started reciting poetry now they'd think you'd gone off your head.'

'Everything changed,' I said. 'And you gave it up.'

'No,' he said, 'it wasn't quite that. It wasn't a question of us giving poetry up. We were forsaken by poetry.'

The fate of Farol is an outstanding example of what was to destroy the extraordinary charm of the villages and towns of the eastern seaboard of Spain, including those such as Torremolinos and Benidorm, once fishing villages with a population living in enchanting surroundings and great tranquillity. In 1984 the municipality of Farol announced with pride that 200 hotels and campsites had been built in the vicinity and that 100,000 guests could be accommodated in these at the height of the season.

In Spain the damage inflicted by tourism out of control has been largely confined to the Mediterranean coast, whereas in France, according to a report issued by the Ministry of the Environment, it has affected all parts of the country. France, it was announced, possessed 10,000 temporary holiday villages, of which 4,000 were unsatisfactory, either by posing serious safety risks or through damage to their surroundings. The report cited a situation in the Pas de Calais where out of 237 tourist villages, only twenty-one took any safety precautions. It stated that in Corsica 174 such sites were in danger from forest fires, usually started by picnickers, which everywhere in the south of the country were on the increase. There was criticism of the degradation of the environment in the vicinity of such villages. 'Wherever you look,' said an informant, 'there is a terrible mess.'

The wildlife of countries attracting most tourists has been badly affected everywhere in the post-war period. In the past, Spanish flora was the richest in Europe. A botanist writing in the *Bulletin of the Alpine Society* in 1972 spoke of mountain slopes in Andorra being covered 'possibly by millions of wild daffodils'. They would have been reached in those days by footpaths, but now there are roads, and retracing the author's footsteps two years ago I discovered that collectors had left no sign of the flowers. Even the Spanish national press is concerned at such happenings. 'Mallorca is a botanical garden on the verge of extinction,' said a headline in *Diario De Mallorca* on 1 October 1995. The paper warned that 37 per cent of the species of plants to be found only on the island had already been destroyed by tourists uprooting them. An attempt to protect what was left had been made by enclosing several hundred miles of roads with wire fences, but the fear was that this measure might have come too late.

Animals are equally under threat in Spain, the rarest of them, such as the lynx and the brown bear, although protected by law, having survived only in the remotest areas. Within a year of the opening of the frontier at the end of the Civil War, the international press carried an account of an incident when bears held up traffic on the main highway joining Huesca with Pamplona. Cars formed a queue and after a half-hour or so the bears ambled away into the woods.

With the return of peace and prosperity things had changed. I made the acquaintance of a road-construction engineer who had just put up an ugly house in the village. 'If it's wildlife that interests you,' he said, 'you should go to the Cantrabrians. We've just built 200 kilometres of new roads up there. The wolves come into the villages to clear up the rubbish at night. I read in *Vanguardia* that they still have bears in the caves at Somiedo and foreign sportsmen pay up to 300,000 pesetas for the chance to kill one.'

Remembering this conversation several years later I went to Somiedo and, finding the caves empty, was directed to Abbeyales, believed locally to be the most isolated and inaccessible village in Spain. People here still lived in the circular stone houses of pre-history, with their animals sheltered in byres under the living rooms ('We need them in winter to keep warm'). Don Juan Fernandez Serra, the priest, was also unofficial mayor and an honorary policeman. From the wildlife point of view, he said, the news was poor. Only the wolves were doing fairly well, but with huntsmen now paying up to the equivalent of £3,000 even for a bear cub, and £1,000 for a lynx, these species were locally approaching extinction.

Otherwise, he said cheerfully, things were looking up. Their new road had opened up exciting prospects for the community, and government officials had promised the construction of three ski-lifts, designed, he supposed, to carry foreign tourists to the treeless upper pastures ideally suited to their sport. There was talk, too, of building a holiday camp to accommodate 250 visitors. If the scheme went through, a *discoteca* was certain to be opened, and there were plans to provide entertainment of the sort enjoyed by holidaymakers in an exceptionally lively small town called Espinareda, twenty miles across the mountains.

I went to Espinareda, of which I had seen picture postcards in Somiedo. They showed a row of gracious wooden houses with enormous Alpine-style balconies but these, I was to discover, had been demolished and replaced by angular breeze-block constructions like miniature forts. Espinareda had three *discotecas*, a supermarket, a police station and two English-style pubs. Graffiti were spreading across its walls, there were notices in English and a degutted car had been abandoned in a ditch. Some trouble had arisen through children caught taking drugs, the mayor told me, but otherwise things weren't too bad. He was bursting with enthusiasm. 'Someone like you from the big city is bound to see this as a sleepy little place,' he said, 'but the population is due to double in five years. Come back after that and you won't recognise it.'

1997

LOVE AT ALL COSTS

IN THE WINTER of 1957, I went to Liberia for the *New Yorker*. Landing at Spriggs Payne Airfield in Monrovia at about midnight, I was told by the small boy who had taken over my luggage that he would not be able to bring it to the hotel until it was light, to avoid the possibility of being kidnapped. A report in the *Liberian Age* the next morning threw more light on the situation. Two men and a child had been murdered to make *borfina*, a 'medicine' manufactured from the organs of dead persons and used as an aphrodisiac and to promote rainfall. The whole business was discussed with total frankness. I learned that *borfina* was produced by professional 'heart men', witch doctors who worked at night, selecting for preference women and children as their victims. It was expensive, but there was no shortage of rich men who would pay a hundred dollars for a scent-bottle full. Heart men belonged to a whole range of secret societies, with names such as the Human Elephants, the Leopards, the Snake People and the Water People; and some to an occult group (popular, it was said, among politicians) which had the macabre title of the Negee Aquatic Cannibalistic Society. The remains of their victims were described in some detail in the press. According to another Liberian paper, the *Listener:* 'We are assured by experts that a body discovered this morning in the vicinity of the airfield had been deprived of flesh taken from the forehead, the palms of the hands, and other bodily regions. Foul play is to be suspected.'

A few days later I travelled north to Bgarnba, carrying an introduction to Mr Charles Williams, the district commissioner, a pleasant and hospitable man who invited me to stay the night. He was in court next morning, he said, to try several cases which he thought I, as a foreigner, might find of interest, and I was welcome to attend. Mr Williams was a devout Episcopalian, but most of the people under his jurisdiction were non-Christian, and in their cases trial would be by ordeal – more suited, he believed, to the pagan mentality. Males charged with crimes would drink *carfoo*, a poison of a mild kind, fatal only in the case of pagan perjurers.

Next morning, following him into the courtroom, squeamishness caught me by surprise when I was obliged to watch the swallowing of the poison. The two defendants drank, vomited briefly, then seemed much as before, and when they were found not guilty and released, I was mightily relieved.

But there was no escaping Mr Williams. The next case was less common, he said. It was of a woman accused by her husband of adultery with five lovers. Although any Liberian of standing, Williams explained, was expected to have no fewer than three wives – each purchased from her father at the standard bride price of forty dollars – the law was very strict in dealing with any wife falling short of absolute marital fidelity. Mr Williams ascribed the woman's fall from grace in this instance to the use of *borfina*, in itself a criminal offence only where a woman was concerned.

A trial by burning iron was to be held in the yard at the back, where we found a heart man preparing his fire. The accused woman and her husband, dressed with extreme formality and devoid of expression, were seated side by side. The heart man pulled a long iron spoon from the fire, tested its glowing surface with his spittle and nodded to the girl, who put out her tongue. He bent over her, and there was a faint sizzle. Someone passed a jug of water to her, and she rinsed and spat and thrust out her tongue for the court's inspection. There were insufficient signs of burning, and Mr Williams declared her not guilty. I asked if her five lovers would stand trial, and he seemed surprised. They had already been fined ten dollars each on the spot, he said, but the money, he assured me, would be refunded.

This is the closest I have come to the real hard core of sexual stimulants, or supposed ones. The softer aphrodisiacs are better known, though in my experience just as fanciful; the irrationality of the search for sexual vigour knows no bounds. Rhinoceros horns have been sawn off to be replaced by plaster imitations in the museums of the world. A whole category of animals in China are deprived of their gall bladders, the contents of which are mixed with white wine. All parts of a tiger are now marketable, including skin, whiskers and intestines. There are regular gatherings by diners in a Hong Kong restaurant to consume not only bird's nest soup, but a more invigorating broth prepared from the lungs of a vulture. In Britain, animal-welfare groups claim in advertisements that Canadian fishermen have slaughtered at least 10,000 seals so that their penises can be exported to China, where they fetch a hundred pounds apiece as an important constituent of 'sex potions'.

But oysters remain by common consent at the top of the aphrodisiac league, despite the extraordinary physical passivity of molluscs compared with tigers and Liberian children. Throughout recorded history, many *bon viveurs* have sworn by them. Casanova, bolstered by their support, is said to have become the lover of 130 women, two of them nuns who rapidly forsook their vows after being plied by the seducer with oysters and champagne. The latter I have no argument with – champagne's useful consequences are easily demonstrable – but aphrodisiac oysters seem to me no more than a persistent and universal self-delusion. I have thought so ever since an experience suffered in my youth, nearly sixty years ago, on a journey by dhow up the Red Sea.

I had gone with two friends in the hope of entering and exploring the Yemen, in those days hardly known in the western world. Permission to land was refused, and shortly afterwards we ran into a storm which stripped away the dhow's mainsail, forcing us to take refuge on the desert island of Kamaran, a few miles off the Arabian coast. The island's principal inhabitants were a tribe of pearl-fishers, who spent their lives scouring the sea bottom in search of oysters and had developed a lung capacity which enabled them to stay underwater for up to four minutes. The diver wore a clip on his nose, a weight round his leg and was connected by a line to a dhow from which he leaped feet first. Having collected the oysters in his basket, he gave the signal to be pulled up. Coming to the surface, he was on the point of suffocation. Sometimes divers were brought up unconscious and occasionally they could not be revived. They suffered from neuralgia, rheumatism and tuberculosis, and tended to have short lives. Their main problem, however, was dietary. The island of Kamaran could not support one blade of grass – nothing could be induced to grow there. The pearl-divers lived on oysters and a little seaweed, and although these resources were said to contain the minerals necessary to sustain life, the local medical evidence was that the divers possessed an abnormally low sexual drive and a low level of fertility, to which was ascribed the fact that one-child families were the rule. If a child died, the only hope of replacing it was for the would-be father to slip away illegally for a few weeks to an oyster-free diet in the Yemen.

Kamaran was then a British possession with an administrator from England. 'But don't you eat oysters?' I asked him, and he shook his head in amazement at the idea. 'In a cold climate and in moderation perhaps,' he said, 'but not here. I don't recommend you to try them either. They have an inconvenient effect.'

What exaggerations are committed even by the most sophisticated of us in the pursuit of love!

I came across further telling evidence against the aphrodisiac properties of seafood, this time on a trip to Cuba in 1960. I was there to interview Ernest Hemingway when I stumbled on a prawn-eating craze that had taken hold of Havana. He seemed to be the man responsible for Havana's sudden rush to prawns.

Hemingway had sunk quietly into the background towards the end of the Batista regime, to re-emerge with Castro's entry into the capital and be photographed in a congratulatory hug with the Maximum Leader. His first reappearance in the press was to lecture the Cubans on their eating habits, reminding them that shortages of rice and beans, the nation's staple diet, were always possible, and that rich resources of seafood remained largely unexploited in their coastal waters. He assured them that the best prawns in the Caribbean awaited harvesting off the Isla de Juventud (Youth), where they were currently eaten only by the natives with a well-known result that had given the island its name.

Of all the many bars in Havana, one called Sloppy Joe's was then the most celebrated, largely because it was Hemingway's custom to put in an appearance there every day at about 1 p.m., accompanied by his admirers. They would then perform the daily ritual of prawn-eating that attracted so many sightseers. I went to Sloppy Joe's one day, and although a bout of influenza had kept Hem at home, the prawn-eating ceremony, Hemingway-style, went ahead as demonstrated by his friends.

The scene was very Cuban. The regulars, their high-heeled boots polished for the second time that day, sat sipping their Hatuey beer waiting for the performance to begin. Two or three decorous and extremely beautiful mulatto prostitutes were hanging about, flapping their fans in the background. The sweet smell of the shore blew in through the open windows, carrying with it the twitterings of canaries in the shade trees. These birds were the descendants of the thousand or two released in celebration of a birthday by the dictator Batista. From the distance another sound inseparable from the old Cuba could be heard – the incessant tapping of drums.

At exactly one o'clock, the door was flung open, and in trooped the men who had come to eat prawns. The newcomers lined up along the counter; the bartender selected a fine and extremely active prawn from his tray, brushed it with oil and dropped it on the hotplate. Here it squirmed and snapped, emitting the faintest of hisses, before being snatched away to be presented on a blue saucer to the first of those in the line.

The recipient took it in a tissue between his fingers and bit off its head. This he dropped on the immaculate floor before he thrust half the body into his mouth and began to crunch. It was Hem's contention that all that was most valuable in a prawn was in immediate contact with the inner shell or concentrated in the underbelly and the legs. The whole prawn, minus the head, was thus subjected to meticulous chewing, and all that could possibly be swallowed went down the throat.

The first prawn-eater did just this, and I was close enough to him to listen to the subdued crackle of the shell in his jaws. When he spat, as delicately as he could, a pinkness of prawn juices mixed with blood appeared at the corner of his mouth. He edged away from the bar, and the prawn-eaters waiting their turn followed. Soon a whitish detritus of prawns' heads and a greyish pulp of shell fragments spread across the floor among the sparkling boots.

In ten minutes, it was all over and time for the serious drinking to begin. But did this manly performance of Papa Hemingway and his disciples at Sloppy Joe's benefit any of them in any conceivable way or delay the process of ageing, as in the Island of Youth? Almost certainly not. The novelist, when I eventually met him, appeared old for his years and, after the jubilant shots taken with Castro, a persistent melancholy had returned to his expression. A year later, at the age of sixty-two, he was to blow his brains out. There had been some talk of mental instability in the press, but this his brother denied. Ernest's tragic end, he said, had been due not to any mental decline but to his despair at the treachery of a body in which throughout his life he had taken so much pride.

So much for prawns.

But what about peas – or cheese? Casanova's formidable record is unexceptional by comparison with that of Ninon de Lenclos, the eighteenth-century beauty who is reputed to have had more than 5,000 partners in an outstandingly active forty years. Asked if, in what is an essentially repetitious process, she ever experienced boredom, her reply was, 'Certainly not. Love may look always the same, but indeed it is new and different on every occasion.' She attributed her outstandingly successful amatory career partly to the assistance provided by puréed peas, to which she sometimes added a little sherry. She was also partial to cheese, which would come as no surprise to an Italian; cheese is one of the supreme aphrodisiacs of the Italian people, if we allow that aphrodisiacs have any real existence.

Italian cheese in its most distinguished form – *mozzarella di bufala* – certainly has most of the attributes upon which aphrodisiacs base their mysterious attraction. It may not quite reach the heights of those witches' brews which tempt the sexually sluggish with their fusion of hope and alarm: 'Take several brains of male sparrows,' Aristotle instructs, 'and pigeons that have not begun to fly' – these to be boiled with turnips and carrots in goat's milk, and then sprinkled with clover seeds. But authentic *mozzarella di bufala* is rare, and rarity (plus difficulty of access or extraction) is the thing.

The cheese is produced in tiny quantities in an almost inaccessible swamp south of Naples by an outdated animal whose ancestors were probably brought to this once-Greek colony in classical antiquity. Because there is so little of it, and because it is so superior to its many commercial imitations, *mozzarella di bufala* is expensive. During the Second World War, I spent a year in the vicinity of these swamps and watched the unsuccessful peasant descendants of a heroic past sloshing miserably through the swamp water to root up the occasional edible plant. The finest present I could send to any Italian friend driven by the disruptions of war from this splendid area was a kilo of mozzarella with all the overbrimming magic that for them it contained.

It was during my war year in Naples that I first noticed one of the outstanding mysteries concerning aphrodisiacs. Why were so many educated men prepared to submit themselves, even if only occasionally, to patent absurdities and primitive beliefs?

Many of my Italian friends had completed university courses. One was a lecturer in psychology, and several were doing well in medicine and the law. Nevertheless, they were superstitious about food. There was the borderline case of the semi-magical properties attributed to *mozzarella di bufala*, which was at least appetising and nutritious, but I found less to excuse the custom of two academics who feasted at Easter time on newly hatched storks, and a surgeon happy to experiment with a soft cheese from Vesuvius to which a macerated lamb's foetus had been added. My friends did not deny that the interest lay in the possibility of enhanced sexual pleasure.

A feature of Naples in those days was a black market of proportions and complexity almost certainly exceeding anything else on earth. Cargoes equivalent to those of one ship in three unloaded in Naples were spirited away, later to reappear for sale in the Forcella market, where even the latest in machine-guns might be hidden under the counter. Since it was well known that this market was operated by the chiefs of the Allied Military Government of Occupied Territories, which was staffed at its higher levels by members of the Italo-American Mafia, it was accepted that there was little to be done.

Eventually I was instructed by the field security officer to carry out some preliminary analysis of the army's losses in terms of quantities and values, and I told him that the most important losses were of penicillin, little of which was getting through to the military hospitals. When he asked me what was being done about this, I told him that I had arrested the principal dealer and taken him to Poggio Reale jail. 'And is he still there?' the FSO asked, to which the unhappy reply was that the man had been freed after three days. At the time of his arrest, he had laughed in my face. 'Who are you?' he asked. 'You are nothing and can do nothing. Last night I had dinner with the general, and if you continue to make a nuisance of yourself, I can have you sent away.'

Since nothing was to be done about the penicillin, my energies were diverted to the problem of vanishing food supplies from the base depot. Here, behind a high electrified fence on the outskirts of Afragola, capital of the Neapolitan Camorra, the local Mafia, several thousand tons of tinned foods were piled high. Lorries came up from the port every day to add to this vast accumulation, and by night roughly the same number of lorries trundled down to the nocturnal black markets of neighbouring towns, carrying about the same amount of corned beef, which had been delivered to the depot earlier on.

I suspected that the eventual destination of much of these provisions was the many restaurants in the area that had recently opened under the stimulus of war, and I set out to pursue this theory. It was against the orders of the military government for members of the armed forces to eat in civilian restaurants, but the most pleasant of them were usually chock-a-block with British and American officers knocking back raw Neapolitan wine and listening to Neapolitan songs about love and betrayal.

Vincenzo a Mare, the most romantic of these places, was on the Posillipo shore under the villa where Nelson had paid court to Lady Hamilton and close to the spot where, after watching the obliteration of Pompeii, Pliny had set off for a closer view of the disaster from which he never returned. It was also here that Cuoca, the last great Camorra chieftain, had been brought in old age for a traditional funeral feast by the underlings who proposed to get rid of him. He was feasted, praised, hugged and kissed by all, and then, full of well-being and at peace with the world, an expert with a mattress-maker's needle stabbed him to death.

Part of my task was to know everybody, and I knew Umberto, the restaurant's owner. 'What are you serving today, Umberto?' I asked him one day, and he told me *frutti di mare*, based, as I knew, on such atrocious materials as sea cucumber and an obscene marine worm abundant in local waters.

'What about *carne alleata*?' This was the Neapolitan term for any brand of black-market meat abstracted from the base depot and served up secretly at extraordinary prices. 'Some of your customers are eating canned meat,' I said. 'This carries a prison sentence.'

He shrugged his shoulders. 'It is brought here by an American colonel,' he said.

I asked him the price, and he told me.

'It is very dear,' I said. 'Twice the price you are charging for *frutti di mare*. How do you explain that?'

'For *carne alleata* we are paying very much, because is better.'

'For what?'

He oscillated his hips in a revolting fashion. '*Per fare amore*,' he said.

'Bring me one of the tins,' I told him. He brought one in a bag, and we went into a corner together where he opened it.

'Spam,' I said. 'Of all things. Spam, an aphrodisiac. Just imagine it. Do you personally believe this is good to *fare amore*?'

He laughed. 'They are all eating it for this purpose. But for me personally – you want I tell you straight? I don't eat any of these things. For me is good wear a medal for San Rocco. This is OK for me. This is doing trick.'

1995

ALLIGATORS IN THE SWAMP

ON A VISIT to Cuba in 1961 I went to see Enrique Carreras, the new air force chief, and found him at his office desk at Havana airport. He was a man in his middle forties, although perhaps in appearance a little old for his years, and there was something in his studious, concentrated expression that reminded me, until one of the frequent smiles broke through, of a friend who studied postage stamps through a magnifying glass. His secretary warned me, 'He's very unassuming. Don't call him Captain. Just say "you".' Chaos still had the upper hand here, since a recent attack by Cuban opponents of the regime flying in from Miami. A chair for me had to be dislodged from a pile of salvaged furniture. 'You see how we live these days,' Carreras said with a laugh. 'Still, things are on the upturn.' He spoke good English, from which I noticed that the Americanisms locally in common use had been expurged.

Carreras had agreed to talk about his personal contribution to the defeat of the invasion attempt at the Bay of Pigs earlier that year. This, as expected, he seemed determined to play down. 'It was largely a matter of luck,' he said. 'They weren't prepared for what little resistance we were able to put up, and it took them by surprise. The fact is that by the time I took over, all the best pilots had cleared off to Miami. I was sad to see them go because we were all friends together until the last moment. The worst of it was they took all the planes worth having, leaving us with the junk. I was particularly close to Rojas, who was chief here before me. He left a letter for me ending, "Goodbye sucker." There was nothing malicious about it. Rojas was fond of a joke. He had his future to think about, but I couldn't help seeing what was happening as the beginning of the end.'

A secretary came in with coffee. She was one of the new kind with short hair, no make-up and flat shoes. This gave me the opportunity for a quick glance round at the surroundings and I noticed a shattered window still awaiting replacement and a door that hung askew. What could have been Carreras's personal possessions had been shoved into a corner, including a fuzzy photograph of a woman with a child, probably his wife, and a voodoo shrine-idol of the kind people now collected, with a fat cigar stuck between straw lips.

'They came over at six in the morning,' Carreras said. 'My first thought was that this was another earthquake. I'd taken to sleeping here to be on the safe side and I rushed out to see my personal T-33 jet-trainer burning like a hay-rick, and the best of our Sea Furies blown all over the parking bay. The bombing was very accurate and whoever planned it knew just what to leave and what to take out. I couldn't help feeling that Rojas was in on this. Somehow or other he managed to knock out the generator and the phones. They're working on them now. You can still smell the fused wires.' He pushed open the nearest window just at the moment when some mechanics, believing themselves unobserved, had put aside their spanners and reached for their guitars, and I listened to the thin, sweet music of Cuba as the flutes picked their way through the background noise of riveters at work. Carreras attempted an indulgent smile.

'Was it five planes you were left with? I asked.

'Three,' he said. 'All of them ready for the scrap heap. We were down to two Sea Furies and an even older B.26. They were suffering from metal fatigue and their engines were worn out. The Sea Furies had defective brakes. The guns on the B.26 jammed and it was doubtful if it had the power to get off the ground. The next thing was that the news came through that the invasion fleet had been sighted in the Florida Straits heading south. That gave us exactly one day to get ready for them.'

'God, what a problem.'

'We called up every spare mechanic in the city and had them working all day and most of the night. No one was allowed to stop to eat. They took rice and beans out to them and had the base doctor mix ground-up amphetamine pills with it to keep them awake. We cannibalised old passenger planes and managed to adapt a few parts stripped from lorries and tractors. The old B.26 was practically rebuilt. I put in a few hours myself to help all I could. At about four in the morning I went to sleep in a chair under one of the Sea Furies, and just before five they called me to say that Fidel was on the phone. "Enrique," he said, actually calling me by my first name, "the sons-of-bitches have arrived. They're landing at the Bay of Pigs. How many planes can you get into action?"

"Three, Commandante," I told him. "Three, well, more or less. If they can be started up."

' "How soon can you get them down to Largatera?" Castro asked.

' "In twenty minutes, Commandante," I said.

' "Good," he said. For a moment he was cut off. Then he was speaking again. "And Enrique," he said, "don't let a single one of those sons-of-bitches get away. Don't let them get away. I'm relying on you."

' "At your orders, Commandante," I said. "They'll be lucky if they do." '

Carreras laughed in a slightly apologetic way, as if on the verge of a damaging admission. 'The truth of the matter is that phone call did something to me. I supported the revolution, but up to this time the leader was a kind of remote figure. I'd see him at a distance in the Plaza making his speeches, but I'd never spoken to him and he'd never set eyes on me. And here he was now, talking to me like a member of the family and calling me by my first name, as if he knew I was on his side. "Enrique," he said, "don't let them get away", and I had the feeling that I really mattered to him and the revolution. "They won't, Commandante," I told him. "Not if I can help it."

'With all the work done on the planes I still wasn't quite sure of them,' Carreras said. He explained his decision to lighten the B.26's weight and to limit the bomb-load to four 250-pound bombs, and the two Sea Furies, now in their sixteenth year of service, would carry two similar bombs apiece, plus eight five-inch rockets. No time had been left for final checks and Carreras's persistent fear was that undetected faults would be revealed at the moment of take-off when the veteran planes were exposed to maximum strain. He absented himself, he said, for a few minutes to write a note to his wife, with recommendations for the disposal of his possessions if necessary, climbed into the cockpit of one of the Sea Furies and noted with huge relief the smoke billowing from all three planes, which proved that they were about to take off.

Almost as soon as he had promised Castro, they were over the Bay of Pigs. The sun had just come up and the sea was patterned all over with ships. To the west the great swamp known as La Largatera began immediately at the edge of the beach, which curved all round the bay and stretched unbroken, except for a single narrow road, all the way to the horizon. Tiny white puffs showed here and there along the road, and Carreras concluded that these were shell-bursts, and that invaders already ashore were under fire from the defenders. In a matter of seconds, followed by the second Sea Fury and the B.26, Carreras was over the invasion fleet. His orders were to avoid attacking any invaders already ashore and to concentrate on the incoming ships. Carreras picked for himself a large troop transport escorted by two frigates, its deck crowded with men, moving slowly towards the beach. This he identified as an 8,000-ton Liberty ship probably carrying, in addition to the maximum number of fighting troops, the key personnel of the operation. It would have been held back until the landing had been secured by commandos already ashore. It was at this juncture that, in an attempt to check his height, Carreras discovered that his altimeter had stuck at 3,000 feet.

Even an experienced pilot found difficulty in judging altitudes when over the sea, so guesswork now took a hand. Coming in for a bombing run at an estimated 800 feet, Carreras ran through the anti-aircraft barrage of a dozen ships. He let go his bomb, missing the Liberty ship by twenty yards, and, caught in a hailstorm of iron and fire, the Sea Fury juddered over cobblestones of air, ducked, wobbled and finally climbed out of range, punctured and ripped in a dozen places in the fuselage and wings. A stray thought of Rojas forced itself on Carreras. The force's top pilot would never have missed.

With a single bomb left and his confidence on the verge of collapse, Carreras decided that his only hope of putting the Liberty ship out of action was a rocket attack at close range under the anti-aircraft fire and at maximum speed, whatever the risk of ending in the sea.

He banked, turned and went into a dive known in the training school as an 'ultra', something he had never attempted before. For a moment he felt weightless, hanging in space; his joints cracked, blood vessels snapped in his temples, there was pressure on his eyes, and iron fingers had been thrust into his ears. At about 300 feet, as the ship rushed up to him and with the plane's nose held steady and pointed at the centre of the cattle-stampede of human bodies, he fired the rockets, blotting out the scene with smoke, before pulling out of the dive and into a sky buttoned all over with bursting shells. His friend Mateos passed below in the second Sea Fury, blasting with machine-guns at a nearby transport, and at this moment the B.26, seen for the first time, drifted backwards into view. An arc of gunfire from which Carreras thought it was too slow to escape had followed it round the bay, and now it simply disappeared.

Carreras turned back for a final view of the Liberty ship. 'They must have stacked up ammunition on the deck,' he said, 'for it was on fire, still struggling for the shore, and dragging with it in the water a black encrustation of drowning men.' He described this scene with no trace of satisfaction. 'I'm squeamish by nature,' he said, 'I wanted to do something to save these poor men, not kill them.' A few, he said, had reached the beach, but there was no cover from the fire of Fidel's shock troops on the narrow road from Cienfuegos, and they were all mown down.

'The swamp here,' he said, 'comes down to within feet of the sand, and a lot of them took the chance of hiding in it.' He sighed. 'I'd been there hunting in the old days, and I knew only too well that there were alligators everywhere.'

1997

BORIS GIULIANO – THE MAN WHO MIGHT HAVE SMASHED THE MAFIA

MY EXPERIENCE OF a Sicilian Mafia trial was extraordinary. It had attracted some international interest, having been widely advertised as designed to lay once and for all the hideous Mafia ghost. Others followed, each more spectacular than the last, with the accused men caged like animals in specially built courtrooms, and the judges escorted by armoured cars from their homes to the Palace of Justice. All foundered in boredom and disbelief, and the secret government of the Mafia behind the scenes continued as before.

I attended this occasion in 1968 on behalf of a London newspaper, and as they had asked for photographs I went to a friend on *L'Ora* of Palermo, who promised to produce a photographer. 'He's a low-grade man of respect,' my friend said. 'You may not be inspired by his photography, but he knows how to handle the judge – which is what really counts.'

Next day I went down to the courthouse where this man awaited me in surroundings that differed hardly in the matter of noise and excitement from a market place. Lo Buono was small and dynamic and bursting at the seams with a kind of genial cynicism. He carried an immense old-fashioned camera and tripod, and at the moment of entering the courtroom where the nineteenth day of the trial was about to begin, we were halted by an usher barring the way. His manner was exceedingly deferential. 'Will you be taking photographs today, Signor Lo Buono?' he asked. 'That is my intention,' Lo Buono replied, and the man smiled and bowed. As at that moment we had been standing under a notice announcing that photography was forbidden under pain of the severest sanctions, this came as a surprise.

The court was in session with the wives and children of the accused men seated in the front row of the public benches. They were strikingly middle class in appearance, the women dressed meticulously as if for a first communion service in church. It was quiet in this room after the clamour of the antechambers and the air was heavy with a church-like odour of hassocks and varnished wood. What might have been a vestry door at the back opened and the eight prisoners filed in, led by a *carabiniere* with a gun. They were attached to a long chain, from which a second *carabiniere* freed them as soon as they had been seated in a double row in the dock, although they were still manacled at the wrists. All the prisoners wore immaculate sports clothes with open-necked shirts, and boasted impressive suntans, despite the fact that some had spent a year or two on remand in that notoriously sunless prison, the Ucciardone.

At this point Lo Buono opened up his camera, walked

over to the dock and took a series of photographs of the accused men, none of whom gave evidence of noticing his presence. Next he photographed the judge, who acknowledged what might have been a routine courtesy with the slightest of smiles.

Now came the most extraordinary episode of the morning. One of the *carabinieri*, key in hand, went down the rows of prisoners releasing each man's left hand from the small chain attaching it to his right wrist. With this, while the judge and miscellaneous court officials turned their attention to other matters, the women and children got up, left their seats and made their way in orderly fashion over to the dock where moving scenes of family reunion were enacted. While the judge wrote in a book, the two *carabinieri* joined each other for a whispered chat. Hugs and kisses were exchanged, and the prisoners groping in their pockets produced sweets for the children and small gift-wrapped packages that might have contained perfume for the wives. I jerked Lo Buono's sleeve and gestured in the direction of this scene, and he shook his head. 'Impossible,' he said. 'No one can take that picture.'

It was the last day of a trial in which once again the Italian state had revealed itself incapable of inflicting defeat upon the Mafia opponent. The Anti-Mafia Commission had been in operation for five years (it was to struggle on for another eleven), but had achieved nothing. In all trials that had taken place it was now assumed that the verdict would be 'not guilty'. Many were abandoned when witnesses for the prosecution retracted their evidence, went into hiding, fled the country or even committed suicide. One or two who had recklessly stuck to their guns could expect to be dealt with in exemplary fashion, such as the prosecution witness in the case of the mafioso monks of Mazzarino, found half-dead with a hand cut off. The contention of the counsel for the defence was that the victim had carried out the amputation himself.

Since it had become pointless to call witnesses for the prosecution, a new strategy had been adopted in the case I was attending. Instead of trying prisoners for specific crimes they were known to have committed, the charge was of 'association to commit crime', in which the prosecution promised to furnish evidence requiring no corroboration by testimony in court. The FBI had worked with Italian police agencies, offering proof that three of the prisoners – the possessors of dual US and Italian nationality – were heads of *Cosa Nostra* 'families'. The report was that they had gathered in Palermo at a time when the drug connection between Corsica and the States had come under police attack, with the intention of transferring the European base of the traffic from Corsica to Sicily.

It was hard to believe that the dignified, even benign-looking men in the dock could be overlords of the world of international crime, nor did their records, according to the defence, lend credibility to this point of view. Several were known for their association with leading personalities of the Church. Two had sons training for the priesthood. Another had paid for the building of an orphanage out of his own pocket. Vicenzo Martinez, the very pattern of a Sicilian gentleman, was a war hero who had lost an arm in action and been decorated for bravery (his citation was read out in court). He reminded one newspaperman of an 'aloof and splendid Coriolanus'.

John Bonventre, one of the alleged *Cosa Nostra* chieftains (he had studied for holy orders in his youth), was head of a charity organisation promoting the welfare of Italian immigrants in the States. He treated the court with exaggerated respect, dropping a 'Your Excellency' into his interchanges with the judge sometimes twice in a sentence. He was also inclined to moralise. At one point the judge commented on the anxiety revealed in an intercepted letter sent by Bonventre to an American mafioso.

Bonventre: 'Your Excellency, I was worried about the times we live in. You can't pick up a paper without reading about some terrible thing . . . I always say a quiet conscience is a man's dearest possession, Your Excellency, I'm sure you would agree with me.'

Judge: 'Not quite so much philosophy.'

With that, on 25 June 1968, the trial ended with the clearance of all the accused for lack of proof, and their subsequent release. That afternoon I saw an enraged Colonel Giuseppe Russo of the *carabinieri*, who had been sent from Milan to conduct an all-out war on the Mafia and to see to it that the accused men were not able to slip through the fingers of the police. He was a man of the north, handsome, clean-cut, frank, and with a take-it-or-leave-it manner. His office betrayed a liking for military order of a severe kind, with handcuffs – made to his own design, he confided – used as a paperweight on his desk. Contempt for the Sicilian environment in which he now found himself oozed from him. He referred to the Mafia as 'an oriental conspiracy fostered by local interests'. 'I have been sent here to finish it off,' he said 'and that I propose to do.

'The Mafia feeds on respect,' he continued. 'They have been able to convince people that they are all-powerful, and our first step is to destroy this legend. This must be done by public humiliation. Take the case of Coppola [one of the three *Cosa Nostra* chiefs]. The custom here is to carry out arrests at night. I sent two men for him at the time of day when the neighbours would be about to see what happened. They chained him up and dragged him away. He lost face. For him things will never be quite the same.'

I called on Boris Giuliano, chief of the *Pubblica Sicurezza* of Palermo, whose collaboration in bringing the recent case Russo had referred to in an offhand and grudging manner. He was a younger man than Russo, lively in southern style, who turned out to speak fluent and idiomatic English with a London accent and vocabulary, picked up, he cheerfully informed me, while working illegally as a waiter in various Soho restaurants. He was clearly happy to talk to an Englishman. Giuliano was even franker than Russo and it was soon evident that he was no more impressed with the new arrival from Milan than the colonel had been with him. He was particularly horrified at the account of Coppola's arrest. 'Russo's signed his own death warrant,' he said. 'They'll let things ride for a bit. Give the dust time to settle, then take him out. I give him five years.'

'What would you have done?'

'I'd have turned up in a plain car, been very polite, and given him a half-hour to get his things together. If there'd have been a woman around, I'd have bowed and apologised for the intrusion, and any kids in sight would have had a pat on the head. This is the way we play it. To Coppola I might have said, "You lead your life, I lead mine. I have to do what I'm told." This man only has to lift a finger to have you snuffed out.'

'There was some talk in our papers about smashing the Mafia this time,' I said.

'You can't,' he replied. 'At best you can contain it, which is at least something. It's the way of life down here, and to some extent we're all in it. Supposing you ran a charity organisation and somebody came to you with an offer of tens of millions of lire to build an orphanage. Would you ask him where the money came from? Do you believe the bishop is going to investigate any suspiciously large contribution to Church funds? They call that buying in. You heard about the project to build a marina? This is extortion money being laundered through the banks. When you have a national bank working with the Mafia, what are we supposed to do?'

There was a moment of confusion in the office. He was called away and came back saying he had to go out, but would like to see me again. I told him I would be staying on a couple more days, and gave him the name of my hotel, and it was left that he'd give me a ring and pop over if he could.

Next morning he turned up at my hotel and we went down to the bar for a coffee. Sicilians who live at home in semi-darkness behind shuttered windows appreciate the maximum of light when they go out to relax. This place, despite the hour, was ablaze with the glitter of chandeliers. It went in for Empire-style gilt furniture, which Sicilians also like. The waiters were uniformed in scarlet and gold braid, like hussars, and the service was fast and good.

Boris Giuliano made it clear that he approved. 'And what do you think of it?' he asked.

'No complaints,' I said.

'In Milan they tell you to empty the boot of your car and leave it unlocked. None of that nonsense here. Nobody will touch a thing. For what they give it's cheap, too. They know how to buy at the right prices. This is the best hotel on the island. Know who owns it?'

'I can only guess.'

'By staying here you're contributing to mob funds. Want to take your trade elsewhere?'

'No,' I said. 'There's such a thing as carrying your principles too far.'

He laughed. 'Well, now you see how it is. You're one of us now.'

He had a couple of hours to spare, he said, and wanted to show me the sights. It came up that I'd been in Palermo before. When? he wanted to know. Five years before, I told him. 'You won't recognise it,' he said. 'Nobody could.'

We drove up to the end of the Maqueda for a view of the new Palermo, rolling through the low hills in a great red tide of bricks into and over the grey city. 'Fifty construction companies are working out there,' Boris said, 'with a man of respect on every board. They have the planning department in their pockets.'

'So they're taking over the city?'

'Yes, but if they didn't the Roman banks would, and the money would be siphoned off to Rome. This is a very complicated situation. The Mafia puts down petty crime and it makes work. It's found jobs for 30,000 so far. Kids who used to live on bread and olive oil now eat meat. The inescapable fact is it has its uses.'

'This used to be a beautiful town,' I commented.

'It still is where the developers have been kept out,' he said.

We turned back and parked in an alleyway behind the Quattro Canti, still the noblest of road intersections, and set out into the back streets winding eventually down to the sea. For the moment, the men changing Palermo were too absorbed in the new city to spare time and energy for the transformation that would sooner or later follow here. A cupola left by the Arabs lay cracked like an eggshell in a forgotten garden, where water running in a marble conduit showed through a filigree of leaves. Lizards darted in and out of the cracks in a Norman wall, and someone strummed on a mandolin against the fading rumpus of traffic. We found a bar down by the fish market into which legless ex-soldiers, face downwards on boards, dragged themselves by their hands to be fed by fishermen with the contents of sea-urchins. Nowhere could the heartlessness and the compassion of the Mediterranean have been more bitingly presented. Our presence went unnoticed: no one would listen in.

'All the books tell you the same thing,' Boris said. 'We're in the unique position of an island that's been invaded and conquered by foreigners six times in succession. Every fresh batch of foreigners changed the laws, which meant laws ceased to exist. We've been slaves to six masters. They left us with nothing. The Mafia had to exist. It defended us, fought for us, then conquered us. Now we've been conquered a seventh time. We got rid of the others, but we'll never get rid of this lot, because they speak the language. They're not foreigners. They're us.'

Sicilians are lonely. The sense of isolation from which so many of them suffer sets them apart from the other races of Europe. It is a trait manifesting itself in a number of ways. There are no country houses, and no small villages on the island. People live in towns, where, much as they may be inclined to keep their own company, they are comforted by the sound of voices, the sight of traffic, of people in the streets. Nevertheless they are lovers of the countryside from which they feel themselves debarred, and enjoy nothing more than to celebrate a *festa* by driving out into the grandeur of their empty landscape for a picnic and the collection of wild flowers, to which they are addicted. The problem then arises where to pull off the road. Drivers cruise along on the lookout for a pleasant spot, but also for company. Within minutes of a driver parking his car, he may expect to be joined by another. Each party, pretending not to be aware of the other, will get on with the business of lighting a barbecue fire and fetching water from a nearby stream. No greeting passes. Sometimes, when no second car arrives, those who have chosen the picnicking site will pack up and move on elsewhere.

Boris Giuliano was yet another lonely Sicilian ruined in the matter of his capacity to resist loneliness and isolation by the conviviality of the years spent in London, then returned to a society where reticence and secrecy were the norm.

He loved the excuse to speak English, which, I suspect, may have induced him more than once to put aside his work, and spend an hour or so with me in some corner of the city where he would be allowed to feed on memories of Soho's Greek Street.

I left Sicily and thereafter we exchanged sporadic correspondence from which I learned of journeys made to the US. It had become clear that the Mafia had moved in to control the traffic in heroin; their secret laboratories now produced one-quarter of the world's supply. It was no longer possible for a policeman to continue to stand on the sidelines and talk about containment. On one occasion when he made a brief stopover in London I met him for an hour or so at the airport. He was on his way to Washington to confer with the FBI, and mentioned that a previous visit had had to do with the assassination of President Kennedy, when he had put the theory, later accepted by many Americans, that contrary to the findings of the Warren Commission, this had been organised by the Mafia. His contentions suggested the plot of a novel which I subsequently wrote about the assassination.

In the early part of 1979, Boris's letters stopped, due I supposed to the increasing pressure of his work. In July of that year he visited Marseilles and Milan in the course, as later revealed, of investigations into the allocation of spheres of influence in the narcotics trade between the US and Sicilian Mafia. It has been surmised that high government officials of both countries found themselves compromised as a result of these investigations.

On 21 July he was back in Palermo, and at exactly 8 a.m., as usual, called in for a coffee at the Bar Lux, a few yards from where he lived. He stood at the counter to drink it, then chatted for a moment with several regulars before turning to go. At that moment there were about twenty customers, only one of whom could be traced by the police to give an account of what happened next. 'I noticed a man who was trembling,' this undoubtedly reluctant witness said. 'He was white in the face. He must be ill, I thought. My first impulse was to offer to help. When the *commissario* went towards the door the man followed him. He drew a pistol and shot him three times in the neck. Signor Giuliano fell face downwards, and the man then fired four more bullets into his back.'

The blundering and impetuous Colonel Giuseppe Russo had gone blindly to the attack of an opponent he did not understand. He had arrested suspects by the hundred, nearly all of whom were released through lack of evidence, thus surrounding himself with implacable enemies who were prepared to bide their time. This came in July 1977 when a phone call the colonel had been awaiting summoned him to a mysterious rendezvous. He was heard to say to the subordinate he called, 'This is the breakthrough', before the two men dashed off. The bodies of both men, riddled with bullets, were discovered in a remote part of the island some days later.

Despite his long experience of the environment and the relative subtlety of his methods, Giuliano had lasted only another two years, almost to the day. He was accorded in death the extraordinary civic accolade of *Cadavere Eccelente*, with which only six (including Russo) had been honoured in the decade, and was carried to the grave in a hearse drawn by twelve horses. By subsequent accounts of his career, he may have come as near as any single man could have done to breaking the stranglehold of the Honoured Society.

1989

BEAUTIFUL BEAN-STEW FACES

CENTRAL AMERICA HAS been frequently referred to by its great northern neighbour as the States' backyard, and the undertone of presumed control and dependency suggested by the description has not been lost on the Spanish-speaking peoples of the countries concerned. Porfirio Diaz, a Mexican president at the close of the nineteenth century, famously attributed his country's deficiencies to being 'too near to the USA and too far from God'. Mexico was simply too big to have wholly collapsed under outside pressures but its smaller neighbours, squeezed into a territorial neck narrowing all the way down to Panama, never quite freed themselves from the exercise of Yankee power and wealth. Things for them took a turn for the worse after the last war as subservient dictators were warned against the spread of Communist ideas. Most of these came quickly to heel, but in Guatemala a democratically elected government proposing to defend its liberties by the importation of arms from Czechoslovakia provoked a CIA-mounted invasion and was rapidly overthrown.

Anastasio Somoza of Nicaragua, whose father had

been a lifelong friend of Franklin D. Roosevelt, offered an outstanding example of misrule. In his own country he was generally accepted as an outright psychopath, frequently visiting in person the torture chambers regarded as a normal accessory of such countries; he was even reputed to have installed a dungeon in the basement of his palace, in which opponents were subjected to psychological pressures by the presence of caged jaguars kept short of food. In 1979 there was an uprising against his regime led remarkably enough by Indians, normally accustomed to keep clear of revolutionary action and let the whites settle their disputes in their own way. On this occasion the President's National Guard made the fatal mistake of throwing tear-gas canisters into a gathering of Monimbo Indians performing a 'ceremony', and the Indians, first dressed by their shamans in ritual tunics believed to confer invisibility, went into action, cleared the National Guards out of town, set up barricades to prevent their return, and the war was on. So great a source of inspiration was their action to the rebels' *muchachos* that Monimbo dance masks were thereafter adopted as part of their uniforms.

The Somozas, father and son, had by this time ruled Nicaragua for forty-three years – the longest period of unbroken terror in Latin American history. At his death, Anastasio Somoza was reputed to be the richest Latin American of all time. Among his innumerable assets were the whole seaport of Puerto Somoza, the national airline, the principal shipping line, a chain of luxury brothels in Argentina and one-quarter of Nicaragua's cultivable land. Both Somozas were seen as good friends of the USA. On the occasion of Franklin D. Roosevelt's meeting with the father, the American President had rebuked a member of his entourage who referred to Somoza as 'no better than an assassin'. In a much-quoted reply the President corrected him, 'Sure he's a sonofabitch, but he's our sonofabitch.'

The fighting started by a band of Indians spread to all parts of the country and continued for three years, provoking innumerable massacres, in the course of which an estimated 5 per cent of the civilian population died, approximately half of these being women who had taken up arms in the Sandinista cause. In 1979 Somoza deserted his followers and fled the country to meet his end in Paraguay. Here, while taking part in a parade in his honour, he was blown in half by a bazooka shell fired from a nearby building, being the 105th Latin American president to die by violence in the twentieth century. Left to its own devices, his army disintegrated. The Nicaraguan air force sprayed the coffee and tobacco crops before decamping, while the National Guard took over the nation's fishing fleet and sailed away, and the Sandinista regime came into being.

Visiting the country on behalf of a Sunday newspaper in 1982, some two years after the débâcle, I found that the only car for hire in the capital, Managua, was a glittering American monster, previously the property of a captain in the National Guard. This unique vehicle attracted curious glances everywhere and sometimes a small crowd. It possessed a powerful radio, and whenever held up by collapsed buildings, a bridge under repair or deep holes in the road, I tried to curry favour with the onlookers by blasting out revolutionary songs. The device was successful but not for the reasons intended. In reality most of the audience had had enough of music of this kind, and soon drifted away.

I drove the absurd car out of town and into a beautiful landscape of forests, volcanoes and lakes, and occasional villages painted in all colours tucked into crevices of the red earth. Some of the houses had shell-holes in their walls, and one or two had lost their roofs. A single village sported a café. 'Come in,' said a woman standing at the door. 'Stewed beans are available. One bowlful per person.' This was good news, for so far that day I'd made do with coffee substitutes and a hunk of maize bread.

I followed her in and she put a bowlful of stew in front of me and I tried a cautious spoonful. It was the national diet these days and the taste was at first sweet, leaving thereafter a lingering sourness at the base of the tongue. Many people I was told were obliged to eat nothing but this for days on end, but after the second spoonful I pushed the bowl away. The woman was watching me and I shook my head and smiled, ashamed at this wastage of precious food.

There was a row of bullet holes in the counter, and I stuck the tip of my finger in one of these. 'It's nothing,' the woman said. 'They were fighting round here for three months. A battle a day. For us it made a change. If you live here it's the boredom that finishes you off. Anything for a little excitement. We got used to the war. I hate to say this, but in a way I suppose we miss it.' There was a cripple in the street outside dragging himself along on his hands and knees, the result, the woman said, of a newly invented torture causing permanent distortion of the limbs. The new government had supplied the 'victim placard' hanging from his neck, appealing to members of the public to come to his aid readily upon request.

After this excursion it was back to Managua – a city that had never been given time to rouse itself from the coma into which it had fallen after the earthquake of 1972 before the coming of the revolution and war. Many who saw it at the time were reminded of pictures of Hiroshima, but now the eerie emptiness of the once bustling city centre was emphasised by the survival of the stark tower of the Bank of America and the disjointed mass of the theoretically earthquake-proof International Hotel. A few pedestrians were picking their way delicately through the rubble as if in fear of its colonisation by snakes. Space had been cleared round four burnt-out tanks, left where they were to encourage children to play in them, but there were no children in sight.

What interested me was a remarkable newly constructed air-raid shelter in the shape of a tall and slender isosceles triangle of steel, and when I stopped in what had once been the main street to photograph it, a policeman extricated himself from its base to prohibit this. 'Photography forbidden,' he said, politely enough, with no trace of menace in his manner. He was quite happy to talk about the tower, describing it as an example of the inventive skills of the new Nicaragua. 'Its shape prevents its demolition by the bombs of the attacker,' he said. 'Note that it is sharp at the top and therefore almost impossible to hit. A bomb that only just misses will slide down its steep side and bury itself in soft earth. We Sandinistas shall fight off attack from wherever it comes.'

I praised the inventiveness of its makers and immediately we were good friends. There was a hot wind and the street was full of the scent of dust and ancient fires.

Tiny drops of sweat had formed on the sides of the policeman's nose and we both covered our nostrils against a white air-borne cloud, twisting slowly as it wandered by. The policeman was staring at the Cadillac, clearly fascinated, although under obligation to disapprove. '*Es obsceno,*' he said, and I was quick to agree.

'I know it's obscene,' I said, 'but I was sent here by a newspaper, and I have to get around. This isn't my choice.'

He laughed. 'My advice is to take it to a gas station and get them to smear sump oil over it.'

'I'll do that,' I said. 'Anywhere I can find something to eat on the way?'

'Place just down the road,' he said. 'I have to warn you this is Monday, so it's bean stew.'

'I was afraid so,' I told him.

'Cheer up,' he said. 'They promise us meat by the end of the week.'

Two nurses from the hospital came past, swinging their arms like soldiers to let it be known that they, too, had carried guns. Suddenly I noticed how attractive girls had become since the days, as I remembered them, when young females over-ate to become plump in accordance with male taste of those times. Now starvation, suffering – even sorrow – had carved away the flesh, and everywhere one looked a new and refined style of good looks having something about it of the classical Greek ideal had emerged, as Managua had become full of beautiful bean-stew faces.

I watched the nurses disappear among the ruins, then turned round at a cry of exasperation from my policeman friend as, in defiance of many warning arrows, a ragged car with wheels of different sizes roared towards us down the one-way street. The policeman waved a limp protest as it rattled by. 'It happens all the time,' he said. 'They've all gone crazy about freedom, so whenever there's the chance to drive the wrong way down a street they do. The latest crazy thing is that traffic lights are supposed to interfere with personal choice, so they're tearing them down all over the town. They're out to prove we're really free.' An idea struck him. 'By the way, someone's going to heave a rock through that car's windshield sooner or later. Instead of having a guy at the gas station go over it with sump oil, you could have them paint LIBERTAD in big letters all across the front. Now that really would go down well.'

1997

A GODDESS ROUND EVERY CORNER

DAWN SPREADS A glacial calm over the waters of Cochin, and slowly a muted profile of temples, godowns and palms emerges from the mist-bound promontories and islands over which the city is spread. Fishing boats styled in remotest antiquity slide with their patched sails past the Malabar Hotel gardens, as if dragged by ropes across a stage. The thick-leaved trees release their morning crows, and at 7 a.m. on the dot each member of the hotel staff is at his post to greet the passing guest with a sonorous 'Good morning, sir,' (or 'madam'), which sounds like a salutation and blessing combined. The greeting is repeated *ad infinitum* as often as you pass, until the stroke of midday, when afternoon comes officially into its own.

At eight o'clock a Mr Williams, a guide supplied by a friend, arrives to show me the sights of this most ancient city on India's south-west coast: a small, dark-skinned man with a beautifully carved face and spiritual expression who, having introduced himself, advises me that he is a Christian, a history graduate, and that he voted for the Congress Party at the recent election. His wife is a

Hindu and a supporter of the Communists, who are at present in power in Kerala. 'She cherishes the belief,' he says, 'that Lenin was an incarnation of Vishnu. If such credence is keeping her happy, why should we worry?'

The seeing of sights is unavoidable – a matter of common courtesy as well as of interest. Our tour was to begin with St Francis's Church, started in 1502, soon after the Portuguese had established a trading station here – the first church to be built in India by Europeans. We set out for it on foot by the road to the Willingdon Island Bridge (which links the island with Mattancheri), and thence to Fort Cochin. In the event it was the experience of this morning walk that counted: the clamour and the colour of the narrow streets; the sight of the morning train from Alleppey shouldering aside the buffaloes and the egrets on the tracks; the field packed with circus elephants; the auto-rickshaws charging through glinting laterite dust; the limbs thrust through the windows of jam-packed buses, the rampaging juggernauts, the suicidal cyclists; the resigned cows locked into the streams of embattled traffic; the crashing outcry from the cinema loudspeakers on every corner. A bus station released a flock of office-bound girls into the street ahead; as they came towards us swathed in their multicoloured saris, their feet, concealed in stirrings of dust, seemed hardly to move. A man hosed down a truck painted all over with tigers. An old election poster depicted the fathers of Marxist socialism sitting garlanded under ceremonial umbrellas. Surely these were the sights I had come to see?

The Church of St Francis came into view in an oasis of space within what must be one of the densest concentrations of humanity on earth. When they took over from the Dutch (who had in turn replaced the Portuguese) at the end of the eighteenth century, the British tried with some success to create an image of rural England from which crowds were banished. Here was the village green, the peace, the shade, the large houses in their gardens behind high walls. The church is vast and solid, with an empty tomb that once held the bones of Vasco da Gama.

Three church officials are ready to greet occasional visitors, to display the palm-leaf authorisation ill-advisedly given by the Raja of the day, permitting the Portuguese to settle here. Inside a harmonium wheezes softly out of sight. Outside only the crows disturb the silence, and a few mild cows crop the blond stubble where once there was a cricket pitch. Here, one draws in the aroma of the past with every breath.

The Chinese fishing nets, on view all along the shore from where we stood, were another of the sights. Nets like these were brought to Cochin at the time of Kublai Khan, and the ones I saw were identical in their spindly construction and mode of operation to those still found in less advanced parts of the Chinese homeland. Stretched between claws of wood, they seemed suspended like the flowers of a monstrous blue convolvulus over the sea. At short intervals, when the tide was in, each net would be lowered into the water, then hauled back by the team straining at the levers to disclose a pouchful of tiddlers, worth a rupee or so, which would be split six ways. Across the water, on Willingdon Island, a saccharine Portuguese church with three baroque towers sparkled among the palms. 'The fishermen are all Christians,' Mr Williams said, 'and are very poor. They are showing a lesson in devotion in money spent on places of worship.'

The city is, in effect, a show-window of religions and sects. The earliest Christians were here, followed by Arabs newly converted to Islam, although both were preceded, it is claimed, by 'black' Jews, who arrived as refugees after Nebuchadnezzar's occupation of Jerusalem in 587 BC. There is no solid evidence to support the contention that Christianity came over with St Thomas the Apostle in AD 52, but Syrian Orthodox churches were established by the sixth century, and many of them are still active and independent of Latin Catholicism.

The present synagogue, built in 1568 and the oldest in the Commonwealth, is embedded in a crooked street of spice merchants in the heart of the city: a tiny, polished jewel of a building with a floor of unique Chinese tiles flooded with the bluish light of antique Belgian lamps. At a favourable moment back in the tenth century, the community was so powerful that King Ravi Varma seems to have considered sanctioning the creation here of a Jewish state in miniature, for he presented their leader with copper plates engraved with title to a substantial grant of land. Nothing came of the project. In later centuries the tolerance of native rulers was replaced by the Inquisition-bolstered fanaticism of the Portuguese, and prosperity, prestige and numbers began to dwindle. In recent years emigration of the young to Israel has brought the Jews of Cochin to the brink. One guidebook put their numbers at about fifty, a figure that had declined by the time of our visit to twenty-seven, drawn from seven families. There is no longer a rabbi and, although all the elders are qualified to perform religious offices, it is sometimes necessary to borrow visitors of the Jewish faith to make up the minimum of fifteen worshippers without which the Saturday service cannot be held.

Whenever tourists congregate and linger – as they do in these historic surroundings – attempts are made to engage their interest in performances of a kind abhorrent to the authorised image of India today. Few spectacles in the Orient attract foreign onlookers as surely as the common one of indignities inflicted upon snakes, and it was inevitable that the immediate vicinity of the synagogue should be viewed as prime territory for this kind of entertainment. One operator would hold up a passer-by long enough for a second to rake a cobra out of its tiny basket and subject it to the attack of a mongoose on a leash. The performance – since it was repeated several times a day – was necessarily a listless one. The cobra uncoiled itself with evident reluctance, spread a flaccid hood, and the mongoose, shuffling backwards and forwards in a desultory fashion, finally caught it briefly by the neck before a blow with a stick compelled it to release its hold. Onlookers who appeared to approve were rewarded with the promise of a treat in which the mongoose would be fed a live mouse. Indians, who on the whole are kind to animals, stand aloof from such spectacles.

There were more cobra and mongoose pitches outside the Mattancheri Palace, built in the rectilinear European style of the day and presented in 1558 by the Portuguese to the Cochin Raja Veera Kerala Varma, in the expectation – which was to be fulfilled – of a valuable *quid pro quo* in the matter of concessions. It is now a museum of a sort, housing in the Durbar Hall a display of the Cochin Rajas' ceremonial gear.

The murals with which the palace is densely painted

throughout are regarded as outstanding examples of the Indian art of the period: allegorical scenes, based largely on the stories of the *Ramayana*, but accepted as illustrating aspects of the court life of the seventeenth century in which they were completed. Inevitably those decorating the walls of the harem attract the greatest interest.

The problem of fertility or its lack seems to have been easily disposed of. The wonder drug of the day, *payasa*, was freely supplied by a powerful monk. King Dharatha's three wives (one fair, one medium and one black) conceived promptly and were brought to bed of three strapping boys – each destined to become a hero of the *Ramayana*. The King looks on exultantly while the meticulously painted processes of birth take place. Eroticism in Indian art produces problems of excess and confusion. The viewer is confronted with unnatural agility and a baffling confusion of torsos and limbs. Which leg and which arm belongs to whom? (Eight of the arms belong to Shiva.) Among the gods and their paramours depicted in athletic strivings on these walls, only Krishna, lord of forests and music, is instantly identifiable, engaged in amorous dalliance while playing the flute – with the dexterity to be expected of a god who in one incarnation or another possessed 10,000 wives.

Not long ago a ban on photographs of these goings-on had been imposed. But why should this be? Was it possible that such scenes of legendary self-indulgence could be in any way linked with snake and mongoose acts as a reflection of an unprogressive past? If so, how long would it take for a request in writing, in proof of serious purpose, for a photographic visit to the old harem to be approved?

A call at the State Tourist Office reinforced my worst suspicions. Permission to take photographs might be granted in special circumstances, said the man in charge, but application had to be made to Delhi, which could be expected to take three months to reach a decision. This seemed to be the moment to enquire about the possibility of visiting the shrine of Bhagavathi, some twenty miles away at Chottanikara, celebrated all over India as the Temple of Exorcism, where persons suffering from mental disorders are treated by an energetic form of psychotherapy based on song and dance. The official's response was guarded. After a moment's reflection he said, 'I am hearing of this place, but it is only for inspecting the exterior. Entrance prohibited for foreigners.'

Nevertheless, a taxi driver from the rank at the Malabar Hotel saw no obstacle to the visit. There was something special about the hotel's Ambassador taxis which, despite appearing like all others to be copies of the Morris Oxford of about 1953, gave the sensation of concealed power in their corpulent bodies. They were fitted (unnecessarily one would have supposed) with fog lamps and police-style revolving blue lights. Perhaps there was something special about the number plates, too, for traffic blocks opened up and dispersed in magical fashion at their approach. The driver imposed his own conditions: one hundred rupees, a half-hour's waiting on arrival and no camera-showing at the temple. OK? By this time Mr Williams had left. I was at the driver's mercy, and agreed to listen to his terms. He lit a joss-stick, stuck it in a holder, and we set off down the traffic-choked country lanes, along the banks of canals dense with Chinese nets, then tearing into a market crowd, scattering both buyers and sellers, but slowing to negotiate our passage round an introspective and unbudging Brahminy bull.

The temple was an unimpressive building at the end of an approach glutted with foodstalls and souvenir booths. In India, religious observance and discreet fun mingle easily, and most of those who visit temples enter the presence of their gods in holiday spirit. Devotees and visiting patients were arriving by the busload, engulfed instantly in a swarm of beggars, astrologers and sellers of shrine decorations, of ear-splitting rattles for children, paper windmills and sweets packed in bird-shaped containers which actually flapped their wings.

A trayful of plastic busts of Karl Marx, adorned with garlands of real flowers, attracted the driver's attention. He bought one, then led me to an office where a man in uniform with a severe expression regarded me with evident mistrust. A muttered discussion followed. The driver was conciliatory and persuasive, and we were waved through into the temple compound. The large open space was crowded. In Cochin a goddess waits round every corner, and people came here not only to pay their respects to the goddess of the insane, but for the performance of marriages and a great variety of small ceremonies, such as the feeding of a child for the first time with ritual rice, and the cropping of a boy's infantile top-knot in properly sanctified surroundings. For the majority of those present, said the driver, this was a pleasant family outing.

Worshippers were streaming through the temple doors into a brilliantly lit interior, though the diminutive but powerful image of Bhagavathi was not in sight. A row of small windowless buildings with bright blue padlocked doors encircled the courtyard. In these the patients – the majority of them young girls – were confined between doses of treatment in which they were encouraged to dance until they fell exhausted to the ground. These remedial activities peaked twice a day, when a procession of musicians led by the temple elephant carrying the idol made a tour of the compound. No foreigners, said the driver, were allowed to be present on these occasions.

By this time it was clear to him what I had come to see, and he led me to a small low-walled enclosure in which five patients, appearing to be girls in their late teens or early twenties, were receiving emergency treatment. They had been seated in a circle, each one with an attendant, his fingers entwined in her hair, and each was rotating her torso and jerking her head backwards and forwards in time with a four-man orchestra playing cymbals and archaic horns. When the rhythm speeded up, the patient's gyrations and contortions increased in violence, so that only the hold on her hair prevented damage to her head against the wall of the enclosure or on the ground. Abruptly the music stopped, and with it the moaning and the frenzy. There would be a few minutes' respite before therapy recommenced. The ancient tree under which this took place bristled with nails that had been driven into its trunk. There were hundreds, possibly thousands of them, each representing the cure which, said the driver, was obtained in two-thirds of the cases accepted for treatment.

At the far end of the courtyard, steps led down to a pleasant, well-maintained garden in which family groups strolled, sometimes with the daughters they had come to visit. Once in a while a stunning report from the recreation area suggested that small charges of dynamite were being exploded in a festive manner. Small boys dashed about, twisted their rattles, played hide-and-seek among the bushes, and went in hopeless chase after the big sombre butterflies frequenting the flowers. A smiling out-patient wearing a crown of frangipani skipped along at her father's side. In the distance the compulsive beat of the temple music had started again. Apart from that the principal sound was that of the crows in every yard of the sky.

I went back to my driver. Together we made a small donation to the temple funds and the men who collected it daubed our foreheads with grey sandalwood paste carried in a jam-jar. The driver asked for a little extra, and this was given him in a twist of paper. He was a religious man, and in the car he spread a little on each of the two idols fixed to the dashboard, sparing a trace for an icon of the Virgin and Child which, thus anointed, he replaced in the glove box. We set out on the return journey, and he offered to show me round the city for a cut price; but I told him that I had already seen the sights.

1989

LOOKING DOWN THE WELLS

I WAS STUDYING the endemic lizards of the island of Kos when I spotted an intriguing news item in a Greek newspaper. This reported an investigation by the police into rumours that women on the small island of Anirini in the Cretan sea were disposing of unwanted husbands by throwing them down dry wells. It was a moment when, after some months of largely routine and statistical work, I felt in need of stimulation and variety. I looked into the shipping situation, finding that there were no ferries to Anirini but that sponge-fishing boats from the nearby island of Kalimnos touched there with fair regularity on their way to North African waters. It turned out that one would be leaving in a matter of days, so I went over to Kalimnos and arranged a passage.

What fascinated me about this story of homicidal wives – and raised so many questions – was that what was supposed to have happened here in the Cretan sea bore a remarkable resemblance to sinister occurrences elsewhere in the Mediterranean. Something of the kind had been reported from an ex-penal island off the coast of Sicily, and while I was in Ibiza some years before, the police had investigated the cases of several married men said to have emigrated to Argentina whose remains were found at the bottom of wells. Here again the wives fell under suspicion, and although the evidence proved insufficient to bring them to trial, the view of the islanders was that boredom had probably driven the wives to desperate ends.

I raised the question of boredom with the sponge fishermen with whom I travelled, but it was a subject of which they showed little understanding. What to us was an exceptional and usually temporary frame of mind was to them a normality to which they surrendered themselves without protest. There were three of them, in addition to the crew of two, all in their forties, with torsos and limbs brine-cured like hams, and given to long hours of silence. They carried a prostitute with them, a sharp-faced waif called Penelope from the Piraeus waterfront, whom they indulged like a spoiled child and decked with cheap jewellery and rare and extraordinary coral collected from the depths of the sea. They spent the three days of the crossing from one island to the next eating, sleeping and making love – the last on a strict rota – in this way preparing themselves for the stresses to be faced when the diving began. There were a few second-quality sponges to be fished in the shallow waters surrounding Anirini, then they would move on to Benghazi to venture into the great depths and fish with the blood vessels exploding behind their eyes and fighting off the cheerful apathy induced by the nitrogen forced into the blood.

Anirini was all I expected it to be: a brief sketching of cypresses and rocks on a glassy sea, silence, whiteness, harsh scents, egglike domes and a slow-moving, calm yet histrionic population, like bit-part actors waiting to go on stage in a Theban play. The earth that sustained life had been brought here and unloaded from boats over the centuries; subsequently it was enriched with the manure of donkeys, which were a principal form of wealth. The islanders grew figs and olives of the bitter kind and made cheese from the milk of their goats. On this plain fare, enlivened in spring by fledgling seagulls collected from their nests on the cliffs, and at other times by the small, spiny fish to be netted in these waters, they lived on in a vigorous fashion into ripe and supremely uneventful old age.

A locanda provided a tiny white dungeon of a room for use by the occasional tax collector from the mainland, and I was the first guest to occupy it that year. It was run by a woman called Eleni, recognisable from the Greek journalist's description, although not mentioned by name, as one of the suspects in the case of the missing husbands. For two days the sponge fishermen went off to dive in shallow waters, coming here in the cool of the evening to fraternise with the locals in the bar. These elderly, tongue-tied, motionless, closely related men accepted the sponge fishermen's gifts of live crabs, which they caught in abundance, tore off their legs and chewed at them thoughtfully. It later appeared that the locals were disconcerted by the enormous Yugoslav watches worn by the visitors, preferring not to be reminded too directly of the passage of time. Once a sponge fisherman turned to whisper to me, 'Now I know what you meant. Yes, this is boredom.'

By the morning of the third day, the boat's worn-out engine was coaxed into life once again, and the three divers, wearing their huge watches, and Penelope, glittering with necklaces, pendants and rings, stood together on deck as the boat ploughed a misted furrow of water across the harbour, making for the open sea once more, this time for the deep waters of Cyrenaica.

I trudged back through the empty, clean-cut light and shade to the locanda and watched Eleni rinse out glasses behind the counter. This she did, eyes averted, with a series of graceful, premeditated gestures. All her actions, whether busying herself with a broom, emptying a pail or replacing some object in its proper position, conformed to the movements of a vestal dance. Within hours of my arrival I had been offered, for the equivalent of £108, a supposedly ancient terracotta statuette of a goddess, said to have been unearthed in an island cave; the resemblance between Eleni and the figurine was extraordinary. Eleni was a Pallas Athena in the flesh, with the same almond eyes, the same long, classic nose pinched in at the tip, the same faintly critical half-smile and roped up edifice of hair framing her face. Stefanos – the man who had tried to sell me the statuette – had been evasive when I enquired into the disappearance of her husband. 'I guess he emigrated,' he said. 'Anyone who can, does.'

Stefanos was thirty-nine. He had smuggled himself into the United States, and worked illegally for five years in a beer factory in Milwaukee before detection and banishment, excluded thus from a paradise he would never re-enter. Now he had settled – with huge reluctance – back on the island of his birth. In season he climbed the cliff faces to gather young birds for pickling. He acted as middleman in the collection and distribution of donkey manure, and he caught the squid used as bait for a handful of fishermen, receiving a few fish in return.

His office of go-between had been inherited from his father, and once in a while he arranged a marriage and pinned the drachma notes on the bridal dress. But now the island's population was falling fast and marriages had become rare.

'How's the investigation going?' I asked him.

'We have one island policeman,' he said. 'He is looking down the wells. We have one hundred wells on the island. Some of them are sixty feet deep. So far he has looked down three. If you want that thing I showed you, you can have it for 7,000 drachmas. Theoharis from Athens was over here when they dug into the cave, but the guys got away with this one.'

With the departure of the sponge fishermen there was a small problem with time. My own watch had ceased to work after a dousing in sea water, Stefanos was without one and there were few clocks on the island. 'Let's go and see if the old man has been fed yet,' Stefanos said.

The old man was Eleni's paralysed father, whose daily routine, followed in public, provided – along with the position and shape of the shadows on the walls – a rough guide to the hours. At exactly 6 a.m. he had himself carried out of doors and laid upon a bed in the shade of a great vine. From this position in the past he had taken pleasure in a view of damascened cliffs dominating a seascape etched on air, the occasional swoop of a raven over the polished waves, and the men far below casting their nets like discus throwers with the faint supplicatory scream that probably no longer reached his ears: 'Almighty God, send me a fish.' At 1 p.m. the old man would raise a hand, bringing Eleni with a bowl of the beans upon which he lived; 3 p.m. was the time for the arrival of the odd-job boy with the bedpan, who would return precisely at 7 p.m. to assist Eleni with the task of getting her father back into the house.

When we arrived on the scene the bowl had been emptied of beans but not removed, and Stefanos's observations led him to calculate that it was about 1.30 p.m. We moved back into the eternal twilight of the bar in which Eleni's white-whiskered cousins, twice- or thrice-removed, were propped, rosaries in hand, like carved church images against the wall. 'All day the search goes on for something to do,' Stefanos said, 'but outside work there is nothing. We tire of each other's faces. That is why arranged marriages are bad, which I say although I have been in the business myself. For a woman this can be like being roped face to face with a stranger for the rest of her days. In Anirini there are no crimes – only illegal solutions.'

We went on a tour of inspection of the wells hacked out by slaves, Stefanos said, in the days of the Turks. The wells were all over the mountainside, most of them long since gone dry, and in many instances the wellheads were covered with honeysuckle, which flourished in the cold, stagnant air breathed out from the depths of the earth. We found two men working with ropes and hooks, while a third – the island policeman – picked over the detritus they had recovered and piled it into a wheelbarrow. He was encircled by a chorus of black old women, and at the moment of our arrival the village priest came gliding into sight, his face carved with noble indifference. 'Ninety-five more wells to be examined,' Stefanos said. 'Here it is impossible to waste time. A drunken man goes out for a piss at night and falls down a well. If anything is found, what does it prove?'

The great heat forced us back into the locanda, where the door had been thrown open and Eleni stood in an obelisk of sunbeams washing out her father's bowl. 'Next week the sponge fishers are back,' Stefanos said. 'You will be leaving us. We shall be sorry.'

'So will I. It's been a great experience.'

'You look at that lady all the time. Before you come here every time you put on a clean shirt, but you never say anything to her.'

'All she ever says to me is good morning or good evening.'

'But you like her very much.'

'I admire her. She's very beautiful.'

'She is the most beautiful Greek lady you have seen perhaps?'

'I think she is.'

'You are missing an opportunity.'

'In what way?'

'You sit here and you do nothing. It would be easy for you to know her much better.'

'And how would I set about doing that?'

'Nothing is possible on this island. Even the stones have eyes. You would have to take her somewhere else. Let us say Kalimnos.'

Eleni turned slowly, bowl in hand, as if placing herself on display in the drift of the bright motes. I could feel her eyes on us. Where was the motive hidden in this labyrinth?

'There would be a high price to pay,' I said.

'There would be nothing to pay.'

'I wasn't thinking of money.'

'What else is there to worry about? You want the

woman – take her.' He quoted a Greek proverb: 'It's the sins we don't commit we regret.'

The island policeman gave up his profitless hunt, but a police launch chugged into the harbour next day bringing a plain-clothes inspector from Khanía. He was a grey, scuttling little man with a smile of the kind designed to screen secret thought. In a single day he questioned all the young widows and those women whose husbands had disappeared, pressing three of them including Eleni as to the reason for their being reported to have dropped flowers down certain wells. In the evening we drank ouzo together. Covering his mouth, the inspector raked delicately at his teeth with a gold toothpick and watched me intently over the arch of his curved fingers.

His life's passion, he said, was sea fishing, but for one kind of fish alone – the majestic and somewhat mysterious dentex, once served only at pashas' tables. When taken, in its last extremity and dragged within inches of the surface, he said, it glowed with a sudden marine incandescence – instantly extinguished in death. This mortuary outburst of colours was the devoted angler's reward. To catch a dentex called for familiarity based on long study of the habits of the fish. It required special tackle, dedication and faith. 'I know where they are to be found, and I go there,' the inspector said. 'Sometimes I fish for days and I catch nothing, but I am sure in the end of success. I am a patient man.'

The sponge fishermen were due back on Sunday, and on Saturday I went to Stefanos's ruined house for our last meal together. Mention was made of the inspector.

'He is from Ioánnina in the north,' Stefanos said. 'A cold place where the sea never warms the land. It is impossible to come to terms with such people.'

'My feeling is he'll be with you for quite a time.'

'Did you think any more about my proposal?'

'Yes, but in any case it's too late. I see the island policeman has moved his quarters down to the port.'

'My friend, you will never forgive yourself,' Stefanos said. He unwrapped a newspaper package and took out the terracotta statuette. 'This is something to remember her by,' he said. 'Take it and give me anything you like.'

I gave him 2,000 drachmas, the equivalent of £10, and when he jumped up and kissed me on both cheeks I knew it was the fake it turned out to be.

Six months later when I was back in England he sent me a clipping from an Athens newspaper for which he had provided a translation:

' "Referring to the case of Eleni accused of the murder of her husband," Judge Costandiadros said, "I am at a loss to understand why it was ever brought. There was no history of conflict in this relationship, and the injuries sustained were consonant with those to be expected from such a fall." ' The judge added that it was not inconceivable that, disheartened by his unsuccessful efforts to emigrate, the husband might have taken his own life.

'My dear friend, this is for your interest,' Stefanos wrote. 'We have been lucky. The judge is almost a neighbour – from the island of Kárpathos. I am happy to say to you that our beloved Eleni is back with us once more and her innocence proved. She sends you warm greetings, and we are impatiently awaiting your return.'

1988

THE SNAKES OF COCULLO

COCULLO SITS ON a hilltop in Abruzzo, on a level with Rome, but across the country from it, under the Apennines. This is a land of dark, lumpy mountains, empty roads threading through the valleys, and nothing in the silent fields to attract even carrion birds. An occasional village is crammed on to the top of a steep rock pinnacle, some half-empty, some wholly deserted. Fragments of the old southern customs survive where there are people. *Guaratrici* (female healers) and *prefiche* (professional mourners) still serve the needs of the local population. Makers of amulets and those who concoct love philtres carry on a semi-clandestine trade. This is the part of Italy where magic and Christian faith are hardly separable. The 'Catholicism of the people' exists alongside the authorised version of the religion.

It is very much a family affair. The saints are still rewarded for their successful intercession in village matters, blamed for failures, and carried in procession to pay one another courtesy visits. Some houses have protective formulae against the evil eye carved in the stone over their doors.

The fame of Cocullo lies in the survival here of a snake-cult dating from pre-Roman worship of the

Angizia, goddess of agriculture and snake-charming in the ancient Marsican culture. On 19 March every year, the young men who have inherited or acquired the intuitions and skills required in the capture and domination of snakes go into the surrounding mountains for the ritual of the annual hunt. The snakes taken at this time are brought back to the village where – treated with a certain indulgence, even affection – they are prepared to adopt the principal role in the festival held on the first Thursday of May, when the procession of the *serpari* (snake men) takes place. Before this they receive the blessing of the Church, and are then 'offered' to San Domenico. The saint – also a snake-charmer in his time – arrived in Cocullo in 996, to take over officially from the goddess. The ritual, however, seems to have continued much as before.

The pagan goings-on at Cocullo seem to have been practically unnoticed even in Italy outside Abruzzo until a visit paid to the village in 1909 at the time of its snake festival by a Mr W.H. Woodward, who thereafter gave an account of his adventures in the *Manchester Guardian*. Mr Woodward arrived as the proceedings were about to start. Making straight for the church, he was surprised to find, a half-hour before High Mass was due to be celebrated, that a number of shepherds were kneeling at the altar rail, each with several huge white wolfhounds held on a leash, their muzzles resting on the rail. The dogs were there to be blessed and at the same time to be 'reverently' touched by a relic left by San Domenico when taking his departure from the village. This took the form of a shoe from his mule. The shoe was employed as a talisman against rabies. An even more cherished gift made by the saint, Mr Woodward was told, was a tooth he had wrenched from his jaw on the moment of parting. Ever since, sufferers from toothache in Cocullo had been able to cure themselves by kissing the relic, attaching a cord to the troublesome tooth and then using this to pull the special toothache bell in the church.

There were more surprises in store for Mr Woodward. Next day the procession took place, and he was startled by the emergence from the church of the image of San Domenico entwined with numerous snakes, and followed by members of the clergy, each carrying a serpent. It seems likely that vipers were present among the snakes carried at this time, for Mr Woodward goes on, 'The crowd hails him with prayers and invocations. Despite the seeming peril, hands are put forward to touch the saint . . . The venerable priest under the canopy carried his votive serpent with no sense of horror as being an evil thing, but rather with a caressing friendliness . . .'

This was all too much for the pillars of the established Church in Italy. The report was brought to the notice of the Bishop of L'Aquila, who had jurisdiction over the region: he went into scandalised action. It was deemed inadvisable to attempt the total suppression of a ceremony that had been going on for over 2,000 years, so the procession was allowed to stay, but other 'barbarous superstitions' practised in Cocullo were banned. Thenceforward no animal was to be taken into the church, and the toothache bell was to go. Also abolished was the custom by which earth dug from a cave in which San Domenico, a hermit, had preferred to shelter was sprinkled round village houses to keep the snakes away. Some years passed before cautious back-sliding was reported. The dogs excluded from church received the magic touch of the mule's shoe that warded off rabies within sight of the saint's image through the open door. The shoe had now been renamed 'the branding iron', and every sheep leaving Cocullo to join the winter migration to the plains of Apulia was branded in the same way. A decade passed before the toothache bell was smuggled back and put into service again, and now, once more, people sneaked by night into the cave under the church to scrape up the soil considered still to be saturated with spiritual radioactivity from the saint's body. It is rumoured that, even as recently as 1986, one or more snakes found their way into the church itself after the May procession, under the pretence of a competition in which they were judged for colour and size and prizes were distributed.

It was a sharp, clear morning in Cocullo on 4 May of this year. The first days of spring had breathed a little snow over the mountain tops but enormous violets showed in the road verges all along the steep climb up to the village. The houses were twisted turban-fashion through the upthrust of rocks, a little unbalanced in their grouping by a basilica that gave the place something of a Greek appearance. Under this was the cave where San Domenico had once sheltered and performed his miracles, but the building had been partly destroyed by the earthquake of 1981, since which the cult had moved its centre to the Romanesque parish church at the top of the hill. This occupied most of one side of the small square, which otherwise contained a handsome band-stand, a deeply cavernous bar and a few substantial houses with balconies.

The *serpari* pacing below were not as expected. As

protagonists in an ancient magico-religious rite there should have been something about them, a certain non-conformity of appearance and manner setting them apart, but they were no different from any gathering of young men with time on their hands in a small-town square, except for the imposing presence of the snakes, some of which were surprisingly large. Big snakes roped round their necks hung down to the knees of well-pressed trousers, and small ones were worn, coiled like bracelets, round the wrists. The snakes, while alert and watchful, were sluggish in their movements. The snake-men stroked them gently and in response the snakes lifted cautious, swaying heads to study them with brilliant eyes, and thrust flickering tongues through mosaic lips.

The snake-men were willing and even eager for their snakes to be handled by strangers, although they were clearly nervous that they might be damaged. A young man in a blue suit, who appeared to exercise some special authority, was quite prepared to talk about his involvement with the *festa*. Alberto Lanzara had been born into a shepherd family – all the men of Cocullo had begun life by following the flocks – but now he was a technician in the Fucino Telecommunications Centre, Telespaziale, off the next exit but one from Cocullo on the *autostrada*. The easy accessibility of this area of snake-fetishism to the temple of high technology made it possible for him to pop backwards and forwards in his Fiat to supervise the collection of the snakes and their care. It was an occupation providing perfect relaxation from the mental effort demanded by his work. This, he said, had been an excellent year for the snakes. The weather (sun following rain) had favoured their appearance on 19 March – the traditional date on which, if disposed to collaborate in the ritual, they could be expected to emerge, wriggling from the earth. Thereafter they were kept in roomy earthenware jars, fed and tended until the day of the ceremony, and immediately afterwards returned to the place where they had been found, in the knowledge that they would present themselves and await recapture the following year. No poisonous snakes were now employed in the ritual, although one of the preferred varieties, the *colubri dalle quattro linee*, was the largest found in Europe. Lanzara understood that his predecessors in times of old charmed snakes with the music of flutes and by spitting upon them, but nothing of that kind went on now.

The arrival at about this time of the pilgrims marked another stage in the proceedings. Parties walked painfully across the mountains from local villages, or were brought by bus from the towns of Frosinone or Sora, where descendants of people who had emigrated from Cocullo had established pockets of the cult. The first contingent, comprising elderly persons of both sexes, struggled up the hill into sight, lighted candles clenched in hands, heads bent – humbled by this moment of the great day of their year. A soft mewing of hymns was smothered suddenly under the vast wheeze and groan of their bagpipes.

Firecrackers exploded overhead and, passing under a beflagged arch, the pilgrims found the *serpari* awaiting them, and reached out to be refreshed by the touch of the snakes.

With this influx the mood in the square quickened.

New faces had appeared; faces sculpted with the long agony of field labour, and the faces of the middle class imprinted with city calculation and stress. The crowd filled all the open spaces, crammed into the church under the firmament of candles, and into the tunnel of a bar where there were thimblefuls of raw spirits on offer with ritual bread baked in the form of coiled serpents.

Midday approached, and with it the climax of the ceremony. A woman who had been couched behind the toothache bell with plastic bagfuls of earth from the old cave packed up and went away; girls dressed in the marvellous uniforms of antiquity dismantled a pyramid of sweet cakes for distribution among the snake-men. The saint's image on its platform appeared at the church door, and with this the crowd shouted all at once – a sound that surprised like a clap of thunder out of clear sky. This was the moment of the blessing of the snakes and their 'offering' to San Domenico, which took the form of dressing the image with their writhing shapes until every part, head, body, arms, pastoral staff and metal aureole, squirmed with stealthy serpentine movement.

The procession began, seen from the square as a slow, twisting advance through the static mass of the crowd. The top half of the image, jerking forward foot by foot, was occasionally blocked from view by children hoisted upon paternal shoulders, upheld arms holding cameras, and the magnificent hats of the police who were clearing the way.

Mixed in with locals and pilgrims were a small number of young men clearly from the outside world, some of whom I had seen arrive in big cars with Roman numberplates, which they parked at the bottom of the hill. As late arrivals they found themselves at the back of the crowd, and now, suddenly, they formed themselves into a wedge and surged forward with such determination that they were able to reach up and fondle the snakes as they passed. And it was clearly all-important for them to be able to do so.

In this, for me, lay the surprise of the day. These men were not here for a tourist spectacle, or for an excuse for a few hours' escape from the world of banks. They were as much participants in the ceremony as the local peasants and shopkeepers, or the pilgrims who were now walking backwards at the head of the procession in order to be able to keep their eyes fixed upon those of the saint. Whatever the credences involved, they shared in them.

With that, the procession passed out of the square and the show was over. Many of those with cars now took themselves off to Villalago, a matter of ten miles away on the Lago di Scanno, where San Domenico had taken refuge uncomfortably for a year or two in a tiny cave over the lake. Like most of the heroes of religion he was a poor man, who had difficulty in feeding his mule, let alone himself. He appears also in the legends as an animal-lover, who objected to what he called fat laymen fishing in the lake for mere sport, and was apt to turn their catch into inedible scorpions and toads. In the close-knit family atmosphere of local religion he is spoken of as a well-liked relative, recently deceased.

A singular fact emerges about this cave, for in living memory (and as mentioned by W.H. Woodward) young children were taken there to bite through the necks of captive snakes. But why? The practices of magic, which so often present a reverse image of logic as we see it, can be strange indeed. The serpent, associated in the Bible with temptation, the Devil and banishment from Eden, appears in the mythology of old Europe in the benign form of Aesculapius, god of medicine and healing.

The cult seems always to have been strongest in the Cocullo area, where a universal medical cure has been compounded throughout history. This *teriarca*, which could be taken either in liquid form or applied as a salve, contained thirty ingredients, one being crushed vipers' heads, and it was on sale by a pharmacist in Rome – who obtained it in Abruzzo – as recently as ten years ago.

In a shepherd community such as Cocullo, snakebite was once the most common cause of premature death. Yet in the festival snakes are treated with affection, even a kind of reverence. The emphasis is strongly on propitiation rather than retribution. Why, then, this massacre of snakes at Villalago? The probable answer is that at this point and even in this place the ancient ceremony in the goddess's honour would have reached its climax with the sacrifice of the snakes.

Whenever such sacrifices – either of humans or animals – were performed, it was normal for the victim to be accorded the most solicitous treatment until the culminating act. In this case a bonus lay in the hope that in death the snake would transmit to the child some of those qualities, particularly sagacity, for which it was renowned.

1989

THE HAPPY ANT-HEAP

THE FIRST, BUT enduring impression of Kerala is of multitudes: people streaming in all directions, filling every street, besieging every shop, forming instant crowds at the scene of any happening – an elephant bogged down in a ditch, two auto-rickshaws after collision, a boy on a hobbyhorse beating a drum. Privacy is unknown, nor does there appear to be any desire for it. Twenty-nine million Keralans are crammed into a 580-mile-long strip of land between the high mountains and the sea on the Indian south-west coast. This state has been described as a continuous village. Its population is packed three times more densely than the Indian average.

A wonderful combination of geographical and climatic factors has spared it from the misery so often co-existent with a high level of the human presence. The soil is superbly fertile, the waters of the Arabian Sea bordering the state teem with fish, the mountains have kept out all but the most determined invaders, and two infallible monsoons renew the rivers and water the crops. Kerala experiences neither famines nor floods, and somehow or other the multitudes are fed.

Apart from the sheer weight of numbers, the Keralan

scene is one of antlike activity. It is the homeland of cottage industry, with people busying themselves in public on all sides with an assortment of small-scale enterprises. To the newcomer an arresting sight is that of the female members of whole families settled for mile after mile at the side of main roads to break stones: the seven-year-olds tapping away with their toy hammers, stylish teenagers wielding four-pounders with accuracy and effect, aged and toothless grandmothers sorting out the chippings into piles according to size. The onlooker may object that stone-breaking machines could easily replace this human labour. To this the reply is, what in that case would all these people do with their spare time? As things are the women pop out in between household chores for an hour or so's work, on rocks delivered to the front door. The operation is leisurely and good humoured, and the girls make up for it as they would to go shopping. The money earned does not rate as an income by Western standards. Nevertheless many families manage to survive in this way. The low income generated can be doubled by the production of coconut fibre – Kerala's second cottage industry. Most back gardens can fit in ten coconut palms.

Kerala depends almost wholly on agriculture and fishing and, being devoid of large-scale industry, is among the poorest of the Indian states with a per capita income of only £80 per annum. As against this the price of most foodstuffs is extremely low. One hundred sardines cost three rupees (12p), and a kilo of tapioca, one rupee. This with a few vegetables from the garden feeds a family for a day. Nine people out of ten live in a village – of which there are over 1,000, with an average expenditure per family on food of 500 rupees (£20) per month. There are no signs here of the poverty and degradation of the shanty towns surrounding so many affluent Latin American cities, or, say, in Calcutta, or in Cairo – where it is said that a half million destitute Egyptians take refuge in the cemeteries among, or even inside, the tombs.

This is the East at its tidiest. The citizens of Trivandrum, the capital, are squeezed far more tightly together than those of Naples, for example, by comparison with which this Indian town is spic and span. Public discussion – largely upon political issues – is part of the Keralan way of life, and takes place in impromptu fashion, crowds gathering as they do round an interesting speaker in Hyde Park on a Sunday morning. The difference in Kerala is that such spontaneous gatherings immediately set themselves in orderly and attentive rows, not only in the open spaces of the local park but on any sufficiently wide expanse of pavement, without fear of soiling the well-laundered garments customarily worn by the Trivandrum populace.

Keralans are famous in India for their political consciousness and passion for argument, characteristics which may have contributed to the Communist Party's takeover of power on 5 April 1957 – the first time in history that such a victory had been achieved through the processes of democratic election. In many ways the political experiment seems to have worked. Kerala spends 40 per cent of its budget on education and, despite its poverty, is far ahead of the other states in this field, with almost the whole child population at school. Its successes in public health are equally impressive. There are more hospital beds than elsewhere on the subcontinent, the infant mortality rate is the lowest, and if you are a native of Trivandrum you can expect to live about fourteen years longer than one of Delhi.

These are the statistics we associate with the socialist world, and which we sometimes suspect of being accompanied by certain disadvantages. Thus, for example, Cuba is the healthiest and most literate country in Latin America, yet in the view of many of its people these gains are offset by the erosion of individual freedoms.

Kerala seems immune from this drawback, indeed it is hard for the enquiring foreigner to imagine that this is a Communist country. There is an absence of assault by propaganda. One sees no posters of stalwart and joyous workers brandishing the tools of their trade. There are no exhortations by public address system or otherwise to greater socialist effort, or targets to be achieved. The leadership cult has failed to take root in this easy-going environment. Keralans come and go as they please – emigrating in great numbers to the Gulf States in search of wages five-fold those paid at home.

In December 1988 Trivandrum was host to the 13th Communist Party Congress, which was generally regarded as a huge and successful binge. The children got a day off school and many of them wore fancy dress. 'We are letting our hair down,' the locals explained to goggle-eyed visitors from out of town. By the time I arrived it was all over, leaving the streets littered with scarlet bunting, which the crows were flying off with to decorate their nests. A remaining picture of Lenin, tacked to a Ganesh shrine, had been taken down, and now stood propped against a wall under an umbrella shading it in token of respect. By late afternoon the sacred cows were back from the side-streets into which they had been pushed, each making for the few square yards of city territory it claimed as its own, where it would settle itself comfortably for the night.

Benefits derived from Keralan reform tend to be played down in the Indian press, as elsewhere. More coverage is given to economic stagnation and unemployment figures. Government successes have been achieved by a better control over existing resources rather than the creation of new wealth. The reforms have, for example, abolished schools without pupils, which had existed purely to give 'employment' to teachers. Nevertheless the charge continues to be made that labour unions have forced up wages to non-economic levels, with the result that investment has moved elsewhere.

A government economist, Dr K. N. Raj, told me he believed the party's election success was largely due to the minor land reforms it had promised, and subsequently put through. An increase in the practice of rack-renting followed by debt default, then eviction, threatened a large class of small farmers with ruin. The Communists promised to reduce land holdings to an average maximum of ten acres, and give tenant farmers the right to buy the land. It was a move that made sure of several hundred thousand votes.

A further view was that the Communists had been helped by the strength of their stand throughout their history against the caste system – possibly the most effective instrument of domination ever to be devised – which in Kerala had reached its ultimate baleful ramification. Here the four accepted divisions of Indian society had proliferated into seventy-seven main and 423 'accessory' castes. These included no fewer than fifteen varieties of Brahmins, headed by the Nambudiris –

accepted as the Aryan purest of the pure – followed by the possessors of fourteen lesser gradations of sanctity. At the bottom of the pyramid the untouchables of Kerala, too, were subdivided into unapproachables and unseeables – the last called upon to warn of their presence by ringing a bell.

Some of the statistics of exclusion were remarkable. An untouchable avoided defilement of a Nambudiri by making a detour when one came in sight of at least a hundred feet – a distance reduced to twenty-four feet in the case of a member of the warrior caste, and twelve feet for persons of lesser caste status. A special Keralan refinement in the scale of contempt was the ordinance by which the 'Children of God' (as Gandhi called them) were not permitted to wear clean clothing.

The father of the owner of a small hotel in which I stayed was by birth an untouchable. In the days before the Temple Entry Proclamation in 1938, which was designed to put an end to untouchability, he was obliged, if he wanted tea, to throw his money through the teashop window, and the tea would be poured down a bamboo chute projecting over the street, to be caught in his cupped hands. This man's son, although still regarded as a member of the lowest caste, had become an affluent member of local society.

An intriguing recent development is that, owing to the spiritual cleanliness they are still believed by many to exude, Brahmins are much in demand as cooks, and our friend is quite likely to employ one sooner or later in the kitchen. The caste system then – whatever its original function – has become an absurdity. The revolt against it spreads and gathers speed. The following advertisements from the Match Makers columns of the Keralan *Indian Express* would have been unthinkable thirty years ago:

BRIDE WANTED An irreligious or moderately religious, beautiful, educated girl for secular-minded graduate government employee. Caste no bar. No dowry.

GROOM WANTED for white-complexioned attractive girl from upper middle-class family of Kerala. No faith in caste system. Individual merit. Simple early marriage. Furnish horoscope.

About 20 per cent of the matrimonial advertisements in the Saturday issue of this paper reflect similar viewpoints.

Christianity offered the underdog a way of escape from caste, although only too often strings were attached. Fishermen had always provided a high proportion of Kerala's food but, although not quite untouchable, were kept in contemptuous isolation close to the bottom of the caste pyramid. They offered an easy target for the early Portuguese missionaries. Almost the whole fishing population switched faiths. The converts then discovered that the Church proposed to take over ownership of the boats and divide the proceeds of the catch on a fifty/fifty basis. Additionally, a tithe was imposed upon the fishermen's share of the sales. It was a system that remained in force until 1957, since when reforms have reduced Church ownership to about one boat in ten. As is to be supposed, fishermen vote Communist to a man; remarkably enough, they have remained steadfast Christians throughout – still poor but much benefited by the creation of co-operatives, which have taken over sales and provided refrigeration plants making possible the export of fish, principally to Spain and Japan.

I went to see the fishing village of Pullivil which, although only six miles from the fashionable resort of Kovalam, is so little known in the area that the taxi driver who took me there had to stop twice to enquire the way. The coastal belt, hardly more than two miles in depth, in which this and a number of other fishing villages are built, manages in some way to have double the population density of the rest of Kerala.

Yet the only evidence of human presence when breasting a low hilltop overlooking it was the triple towers of an enormous Portuguese church, soaring from what might have been the jungle of the Amazon.

Pullivil appeared at the bottom of the hill as row after row of thatched cabins among the tree trunks. In its severe order, its adaptation to its environment, and the absence of any of the visible adjuncts of our days, it gave the impression of being of tribal origin, conceivably unchanged since before the arrival of the first Aryan immigrants some 2,000 years ago. The tall, broad-leaved native trees were interplanted with others: coconut palms, arecas and pepper trees grown for their crop. The road from Kovalam had been stifling; here, under swaying lattices of shade, Pullivil was cool and green. What little tidying-up there was to be done was attended to by crows, spaced evenly like black fruit on the branches overhead, or by scuttling piglets. Pig-keeping is the custom in such Christian communities throughout India – eating pork being accepted as the best proof of sincerity of faith.

My arrival in this place, almost hermetically sealed off from the intrusions of the outside world, caused some excitement, and two young, smiling and voluble young men were found to show me round. They introduced themselves as Ambrose and Wilfred (their names, they said, had been chosen for them by the priest). We exchanged personal details in the customary manner of Kerala: father's name, religion and political affiliation. They were, of course, Communists; fishermen's sons studying political economy at the University of Trivandrum, home for the weekend. Together we visited the enormous church, the playschool (where on spotting us, the toddlers broke into a vociferous version in the local language of 'Goosey Goosey Gander'), the library and the Culture and Science Club – both wonderfully scoured and polished and smelling faintly of Methodist chapels. Next we moved on to the beach.

The climate here was as soft as Portugal with a hint of approaching rain, and a water meadow carpeted with sparkling grass of the European kind separated the front row of the village houses from the sand. In this buffaloes mooched in a languid fashion among patches of lotus and reeds. It was a Saturday and jubilant scampering children released from morning school played a game by which home-made kites were induced to swoop down suddenly over the heads of passing adults – principally fishermen on their way to the boats – in the hope of entangling their legs in the strings. The boats, lined up at the top of the beach, presented black Viking profiles with white tracery painted over their prows. They were of inconceivable antiquity, made of thick teak planks sewn together with coir rope, and, as noted by the Dominican Fray Domingo Navarrete, who passed this way in 1760, no nails are used in their construction. He was taken for a trip in one, complaining that the water entered 'by a thousand holes and although the Moors assur'd us they were safe, yet we could not but be in great fear'.

The fishermen were preparing the boats to go out that night. They were lean men, calm and slow in their movements, and with expressions of great serenity. Each man wore a white cross, some three inches long, dangling from a string of turquoise beads at his neck. The nets used were heavy and enormously long, and had been deposited in piles at a distance of about thirty feet from each boat. A method of folding and stowing them had been worked out by which a team of twelve (the number of the disciples) loaded boat after boat. A man picked up the end of the net and began to walk towards the boat. After three paces a second man took up the net and followed him, and so on until nine men held the net, fully stretched. They began the process of folding it, then passed it up to three men waiting to stow it in the boat. The procedure, carried out in silence and with military precision, was ritualistic and archaic.

With the first boat dealt with in this way the team moved on to the next. It would take most of the afternoon before some thirty boats were ready for the sea. Ambrose explained that the work of stowing the nets, of launching the heavy boats and beaching them on their return had always been shared in this way; so too were the rewards. The fishermen's existence depended on perfect co-operation. 'We have always been Communists,' he said. 'Now we vote. That's the only difference.'

'Do you intend to become fishermen yourselves?' I asked.

The question was ridiculous. How could a graduate with a head full of data and figures be expected to go out and catch fish. Nevertheless there was a trace of embarrassment in the answer. 'We shall be putting our knowledge at the service of the community,' Ambrose said.

'But in what way?'

He shook his head in gentle exasperation. 'These people are not understanding money. When there is a good catch they are buying jewellery for their wives.'

'What should they do with it?'

'They must be learning to save – to invest. They must be moving with the times. The future is good. All the time we are making improvements. But have you seen Kovalam? In Kovalam there are twenty hotels. This is a backward place but I am thinking one day we must catch up.'

1989

WHERE THE MAFIA BRINGS PEACE

SICILIANS LIVING IN the tightly packed, traffic-jammed city of Palermo do their best, naturally enough, to escape, whenever the opportunity arises, into the country or to one of the rare havens of peace still to be discovered by the sea.

Inland, a favourite excursion is to a small town with a relaxed and somewhat ecclesiastical atmosphere. Twelve churches – some superbly baroque – are crammed into the surroundings of the small square. In addition to its ample provision for the devout, the town possesses seven schools, an excellently equipped hospital, and various benevolent institutions. People drive more than thirty miles from Palermo just to stock up with exquisite bread baked in wood-fired ovens and to buy meat free from those adulterations and tamperings associated with city markets. The streets are clean, there is no petty crime – the last burglary took place three years ago. It is a relief to visitors from the city, where muggings happen in broad daylight, to find that here they can stroll in the streets by night in perfect confidence and security.

This is Corleone, made famous by the book and the

film *The Godfather*, and generally accepted as being under the stern and watchful control of a man held in custody since 1974, who is currently serving a life sentence for multiple murders and for being 'promoter and organiser of a criminal organisation', in the maximum-security prison of Termini Imerese. This surely is a phenomenon without parallel in the modern world and hardly in history. Many Palermitans seeking refuge from the bustle, clamour and insecurity of the city have decided to settle here, although once, back in the Forties, thirteen bodies of murdered men were recovered from the streets in as many days. It holds special attractions for families with children to be educated.

If schooling is of no consequence, townspeople in search of peace may opt for Ficuzza, nine miles away, located in Arcadian surroundings under the portentous shape of the Rocca di Busambra, and at the edge of the Ficuzza wood, once the hunting preserve of the Bourbon King Ferdinand II, whose palatial baroque lodge is just round the corner of the single street. It was the ambition of the Sicilian friend who accompanied me on this trip, and who had taught philosophy for two years at Corleone, to buy a house here. Prices are high – for Ficuzza, too, is under uncontested, and therefore pacific, Mafia control. Cars are left unlocked in the street at night while the populace sleep quietly in their beds. Once a day or so, a policeman on a motorcycle may pass through without stopping. There is nothing for him to do.

The Corleone landscape is dramatic, even formidable, backed by harsh mountain shapes, perpetually misted and aloof; a proper setting for the atrocious deeds of the past. Forty years ago the traveller would have been careful to avoid the Ficuzza wood, for it was here that outlaws kept rustled cattle. In 1947 police investigated a deep crevice on the flat top of the Busambra mountain, discovering the remains of trade union leaders and peasant malcontents, dumped there by the feudal Mafia of those days. There are no isolated farmhouses hereabouts. Those who work on the land live in villages, often built in a circle for purposes of defence, their backs forming an unbroken wall.

This is bandit country, riddled with secret caves and hidden tunnels, and the bandits were here from the beginning of Sicilian history to the end of the Second World War. At that time thirty bands roamed these mountains, a pool of desperate men from which were recruited the private armies of the feudal landlords. In 1950, with the passing of the agrarian reform law, these things came to an end. The social conditions in which banditry had flourished ceased to exist, and the private armies had gone. Those bandits who remained at large were no more than an intolerable nuisance, and, with their usual efficiency, the 'Men of Honour' arranged for their extermination.

Many theorists see Sicily's history of banditry interwoven with that of the Mafia as a kind of continuing resistance to foreign occupations – six in all – which never permitted the creation of a stable state. As a matter of routine each incoming regime abolished all freedoms granted by its predecessor, cancelled the title deeds to ownership of land, and changed all the laws to suit themselves. Thus, at intervals of roughly one and a half centuries, Sicilians found themselves reduced to pauperism by some new category of foreigners, governing inevitably through a corrupt and brutal police. Since the state offered no protection, it fell to the individual to do what he could to defend himself, and his best recourse was to join forces with other victims of oppression in the organisation of underground action. Thus, according to the theory, the Mafia was born.

When in 1860 Garibaldi arrived on the scene to bring about Sicily's unification with Italy, it became clear that there was much to be done before the island could be governed from Rome. It was therefore decided as a temporary measure to make do with political remote control through 'families of respect' – which may have been in effect governing from behind the scenes for centuries before his arrival.

The surrender of land in 1950 to the once land-hungry peasantry saw the end of the old-fashioned rural Mafia, now that their function as guardian of feudalism had ceased to exist. Calogero Vizzini of Villalba and Genco Russo of Mussomeli had shared enough power in 1943 virtually to hand over western Sicily to the invading American forces, with hardly the loss of a man. Their kind was now extinct, and with them had gone all the traditional godfathers, to be replaced by young men of quite exceptional ferocity, who began their conquest of the towns.

In 1950, at the stroke of a pen, a Sicilian lifestyle came to an end, and in the countryside the change was instant and profound. The old system here had been based upon a vast reserve of labour; now almost overnight the labour market collapsed. There was no one to sow, tend or reap the crops. Agricultural wages doubled, then increased five-fold, but there were still no takers. A few field workers busied themselves with the tiny patches allocated in the reform, but most of them either moved into the towns or went abroad – and they would never be back.

We had been invited to lunch at the *casa padronale* of Caltavuturo, south of Cefalù, where the land reform had cost our host all but 1,250 acres of his original 5,000, leaving the estate from his point of view no longer a viable proposition. This reverse had been accepted with dignity and good grace. The small fortress provided at least an excellent backdrop for the entertainment of his friends at weekends.

Life in the *casa padronale*, set in the empty magnificence of what might have been a Highland glen, clung to what it could of the style of the past. Power had gone, but its persistent wraith lingered on. A high wall with massive gates enclosed a courtyard in which, when we arrived, a baker was busy at his oven, and servants, formally hatted in eighteenth-century style, cooked an assortment of meats over a great brazier. The servants, led by the major-domo, came forward to shake the hands they would once have kissed. The baroness awaited us at the head of a marble staircase leading to the *piano nobile* then presented us to the guests, all of them speaking perfect English, learned in all probability from Anglo-Saxon governesses. Courtesy titles had been firmly retained.

The talk was of English literature of the nineteenth century, of a croquet lawn it was hoped could be created, and the possibility of introducing fox-hunting in this moorland and scrub environment, so unfavourable, one would have supposed, to the sport. Although the people of the estate had received their 3,750 acres, they had all left, and the heather spread a coverlet over the once-cultivated fields.

Lunch had been based upon a recipe chosen from a selection of British glossies on display, the one medieval touch being that the bread was presented to each guest in turn to be respectfully touched. Strong Sicilian white wine was provided from the vineyard of Conte Tasca D'Almerita, present for the occasion, who announced himself as grandson of Lucio Tasca, deviser of the plan in the late Forties for the 'tactical utilisation' of the bandits into a Separatist army. This, it was hoped, would detach Sicily from Italian sovereignty and offer it to the United States. Ironically, the grandson, as he told me, had been captured and held to ransom for some months in a cave by Salvatore Giuliano, most famous bandit of them all. 'He was extremely polite,' the count said, 'and never failed to address me by my title.' A memory caused him to wince. 'The food,' he said, 'was monotonous.'

Caltavuturo was a quiet place, perhaps a little dull, but in the past excitements had been frequent. A feature of the house was a tower with two storeys. Three embrasures were provided in each room, through which rifles could be pointed at attacking outlaws, who had never succeeded in scaling the wall. Our charming hostess pointed out the six thrushes' nests, one per embrasure, each having five eggs. The thrushes had become house mascots, inordinately tame. Sometimes in the bad old days, when an attack was imminent, the nests had had to be removed, but this was done with great care, and as soon as the danger was at an end they were replaced. Usually the birds returned.

Sicily, apart from the coastal strip in which its principal towns are located, is fast emptying of its people. The *autostradas*, unrolling their ribbons of concrete across the island from north to south and east to west, are largely devoid of traffic. The monks drift away from the isolated monasteries, and the great feudal houses have lost all purpose. Fields that once produced Europe's highest yield of wheat are now submerged in gigantic thistles. Only shepherds inhabit this landscape, and if one makes a roadside stop they come scurrying down the mountain slopes to the car, desperate for a moment of relief from their loneliness. Like magicians they draw the new-born lambs from their sleeves, and unburden themselves of pent-up words. 'Don't go away,' they say. 'Why the hurry? Let's talk about something.'

Nostalgia still drags at those who have turned their backs on the scenes of their childhood and emigrated to the towns, and at holiday time they swarm out into the country to pay their respects at the shrines beckoning in the background of their lives. For the ex-villagers who have moved into Palermo, the most powerful of such magnets is the great temple of Segesta, and, making their pilgrimage by bus in spring, they deck themselves with red poppies in tribute, it is to be supposed, to the watchful spirits of the place.

The temple awaits them at the top of a steep slope, a ravine at its back. It is colossal and perfect although never finished; seemingly part of the present, since it is untouched by ruin. Here the mystery of antiquity is complete, for nothing remains but contoured fields concealing its foundations, and a theatre on a hilltop a mile away, from which it appears as a bright new child's toy. It stands in a wide encirclement of mountains, facing an escarpment of white rock, a black cliff launching its falcons over the valley, and, to the south, the dingy pile of Monte Grande. At the end of the day when the crowds have gone, this supreme monument dominates one of the lonely places of the earth.

Back in the grim industrial suburbs after their brief escape to the country, the new townsmen and women, subjected to a turbulent and frequently violent environment, continue stoutly to defend village values. In Brancaccio, where the police barracks have been blown up on two occasions, and last year eight men were killed in a shotgun massacre, a principal concern is for female deportment. Thus lengths of cloth are stretched along balconies to impede the view of feminine legs, and some doors have been modified to resemble those of a stable. These enable housewives to conceal the lower part of their bodies while chatting with neighbours or buying from passing street traders.

Chaos – the word is hardly ever out of Sicilian mouths – reigns in places such as this, subjected to a divided Mafia engaged continually in mutual slaughter over the division of the spoils. In nearby Bagheria the death toll among contending factions amounted to fifteen in just twelve months. More important to many onlookers is the demolition of this enchanting seaside town – once a showpiece of baroque architecture – by illicit Mafia property development. Bagheria, favoured resort of the eighteenth-century nobility – who threw money to the wind in construction of fanciful palaces – has been buried under concrete. Only the eccentric and exuberant Palazzo Palagonia, with sixty-two ceramic monsters ranged along its surrounding wall, remains intact – and this is certain to go.

In the opinion of many Sicilian experts, the Mafia, with its close and fatal involvement in politics and high finance, cannot be defeated in the foreseeable future. Current tactical problems in the struggle arise from an internecine war resulting in the destruction of strong bosses, and leaving power vacuums to be filled. A case in point is the tragic history in recent years of the town of Alcamo, about forty miles from Palermo, following the sudden death of eight out of nine members of the Riina family, an outstandingly successful firm supplying one-sixth of the US consumption of heroin, besides being a major clandestine exporter of arms to the Middle East. Their elimination following orders from a prison cell in Termini Imerese was a catastrophe for the citizenry, who lived comfortably, more or less as the people of Corleone do now, under nominal overlords who ran their profitable affairs and left them in peace. Anarchy followed the Riina collapse. Those who sought to replace them lacked the capital to take over their businesses and, in order to raise this, have devised a system of protection rackets from which there is no way of escape. An innovatory technique has compelled the banks to hand over their files, and on incomes thus revealed a percentage is levied. Resistants quickly change their minds when their cars or houses go up in flames. Farmers are brought to heel by the loss of valuable agricultural machinery. Since the police no longer count in a situation like this, the unfortunate people of Alcamo can only pray for a return of the old Riina-style stability.

Organised crime has now spread to most towns on the island. Nevertheless, bright spots remain amidst the encircling gloom, and Mondello, a pretty seaside town fifteen miles to the west of Palermo, is one of these. It is saturated with calm, family pleasures. Villas with absurd turrets and fake-antique fountains spouting water from grotesque mouths line a promenade along which carriages dawdle under the palms' spiky shade. Taped Neapolitan music wails in the cafés where customers sit through the day demolishing sculpted ice-cream; corpulent fathers, their trousers rolled up, net tiny fish in the shallows.

Soon after our arrival here on an evening in early autumn, a wedding party came on the scene. The theatrical setting of the Mondello waterfront is much favoured for the ritual photography following the church ceremony, staged in surroundings such as this, as my friend put it, 'to commemorate the event in the public eye'. The quay was instantly transformed into a stage upon which the bride glided on her father's arm. A corps of photographers were at work in the background, moving a Rolls-Royce here and a boat there, in preparation for an instant of extreme luminosity following sunset, when the division vanishes between sea and sky and a lively refulgence touches every cheek. The wedding group formed, and as if at the touch of a single switch, the lights came on all round the bay. There was a soft, crowd-produced gasp of appreciation, the cameras flashed and the audience put down their ice-cream spoons and clapped.

Almost certainly among this gathering would have been Sicilians now living in the States, who had flown over to take part in the feast of the 'Sainted Physicians', Cosima and Damiano, celebrated three miles down the coast at Sferracavallo. Their engagement is a strenuous one, for they join a group of about a hundred who carry the enormously heavy platform supporting the figures of the saints in a rapid, jogging promenade for hours on end up and down the streets of the village. In the course of this, as one devotee after another collapses from fatigue, another rushes to take his place. With every year that passes, the Sainted Physicians draw greater crowds, and the American contingent increases. What is extraordinary is that Cosima and Damiano have no history, and no one knows what this wild annual scamper through the streets is really all about.

If nothing else, it demonstrates the huge and often increasing strength of custom. A Bostonian participant, in Sferracavallo for two days, told a reporter: 'I suffer from depression. Most years I come over and do this, and that does the trick for a while. If I can't get away I phone in and listen to the music, which is better than nothing.' It is this stubborn traditionalism, this inextinguishable respect for the comfortable values of the past, that may provide a last-ditch defence in Sicily against the encroaching ugliness of our age.

1990

BACK TO THE STONE AGE

THE DANIS OF Irian Jaya, tall, graceful and athletic Melanesians remotely related to the Aborigines of Australia, are remarkable among the so-called primitives for their steadfast and successful resistance to the civilising pressure of our times. They rank amongst the world's most sophisticated cultivators of the soil, employing horticultural techniques of their own devising only to be found in the most advanced countries of the West. In this way they provide themselves both with an ample diet and an abundance of leisure. They are notable for their hospitality and good humour and are irrepressibly polygamist. Despite the chill of the night in the highlands in which they live, they wear as little as possible. Bare-breasted Dani women retain the original revelatory grass skirts of the South Seas. Their menfolk, ignoring disapproval from any source, go about their affairs naked except for a penis gourd. This solitary article of apparel, sometimes as much as three feet in length, decorated in various ways, and even dangling a tassel at its tip, serves a utilatarian as well as sartorial purpose, being used to carry items such as small change, a cowrie-shell bracelet too valuable for everyday wear or the inevitable ballpoint pen.

It was June 1938 when visitors from the outside world first sighted the Baliem Valley of the Danis from a plane carrying an expedition led by an American explorer, Richard Archbold, in a flight over the vast, unmapped spaces of Dutch New Guinea. Suddenly the densely forested mountains opened up to disclose a sparkling, and seemingly densely populated landscape. Almost all New Guinea remained solidly embedded in the Stone Age, and Archbold and his companions, who assumed that nothing much had changed here for 10,000 years, were astonished by the precise geometrical lay-out of the fields they looked down upon and a complex irrigation system equalling anything of the kind to be found elsewhere in modern times.

An overland expedition that followed to investigate what was spoken of as a Lost World ran into difficulties. Apart from scientifically minded explorers, it included a contingent of Dutch police, and, for some unexplained reason, thirty convicts. Their reception was enthusiastic, but a problem arose when the newcomers attempted to depart. It has been suggested that the involved protocol of Dani hospitality was responsible for the hold-up. The matter was promptly settled by shooting two of the tribesmen, after which no attempt was made to delay the expedition further. Decisive action of this kind was the norm in the New Guinea of those days.

A year later, the first missionaries who made their way to the scene seem to have been a mild enough collection. The eastern half of New Guinea, then in British hands, suffered from a massive influx of evangelists, most of whom had carved out exclusive spheres of influence and were at loggerheads with each other. In the western half, which was to become Irian Jaya, the scandal and dismay at the happenings in the east led to a religious pact by which the Catholics took over the northern half of the newly occupied area, and the Protestants the south.

Baliem fell to the Catholic Dutch, who advanced the cause of salvation in a sympathetic and even indulgent fashion. The good fathers administered injections, handed out malaria pills, put up with polygamy and penis gourds, turned a blind eye to occasional outbursts of ritual warfare and drank schnapps. There were frequent handouts of such useful things as cough-drops, mittens and walking sticks, all of them joyfully accepted by their flock, who expected no less.

The Cargo Cult, originating in early contacts between tribes and the first white traders, had been slowly spreading through much of the Far East. It assumed that all the desirable objects offered by traders were of supernatural provenance, to be found in abundance in the other world, and readily available if the right religious ceremonies were performed. Perhaps for this reason the Danis enthusiastically repeated the formulae their pastors required of them, and flocked to the mission church, in which they spent as much time as they could, in the belief that beneficial influences could be absorbed through the seats of the chairs.

It was a happy state of affairs that continued until the post-war period, to be abruptly terminated by the arrival of a legion of air-borne evangelists, recruited largely in the American Mid-West, and headed by a Texan, Lloyd Van Stone, who claimed that he had received 'a mandate from Heaven' to invade the Baliem and bring the Danis to God. Van Stone said that he found Catholicism as practised by the villagers to be unrecognisable as

Christianity, and the latest techniques of business promotion went into action in support of a fundamentalist New Deal. The trickle of benefits swelled into a flood, with lavish offerings of salt – the most valued Dani commodity – steel axes and iron tools of all descriptions. A slight change in the formula learned from the Catholic fathers was all that the evangelists at first demanded. Danis switched to Protestanism on the spot, 'witnessing for Christ' in their ecstatic thousands. Don Richardson, a fundamentalist missionary who was there at the time, describes in his book the joyousness of Van Stone's reception. 'Thousands of stone-age people. Singing, dancing and thronging! And asking what must we do to welcome the message you bring?'

The answer was instantly provided. They were to scour the valleys, destroy the ritual houses which were central to village life and bring in for destruction the 'fetiches' they contained. In February 1960 thousands of these, consisting of ancestral figures, carved and decorated shields, paddles, household embellishments and articles of many kinds, were put to the flames. Among them, undoubtedly – as in other areas where such holocausts were carried out – great works of art were lost. The Dani 'sacred objects' were consumed in a pyre stated to have been 200 yards long, a yard high and two feet wide, and thus in a single evening perished the art of the Dani people. One might ask how a handful of whites could so easily have imposed their will upon the numerous warlike and intelligent tribespeople who confronted them, and Richardson unhesitatingly and with evident relish describes how the thing worked.

The missionaries had delved deeply into Papuan legend and, examining the origins of the Cargo Cult, hit upon the widely held tribal belief that the powerful and generous white visitors of the past were none other than their own reincarnated ancestors. These had been changed into whites by death, thereafter returning invested with the authority of the other world. It was immediately recognised as a credence that could be put to invaluable use, especially when the evangelists were in the process of spreading from the Baliem into remote, hardly accessible valleys.

It had been decided that in each valley an airstrip should be built for the use of the planes bringing in supplies and affording emergency protection. Unfortunately, the building of such strips often involved the destruction of Papuan villages and the gardens constructed over the centuries that supported them. However, nothing was allowed to impede the harvest of souls, and the ticklish negotiations involved in such projects were put in the charge of Stanley Dale and Bruno De Leeuw, two missionary specialists in this particular field.

Don Richardson shows the pair in action. They had gone with five Dani converts to the remote valley of Ninia, peopled by close relations of the Danis, the Yalis. Previous research had been made into their history and beliefs, and now, employing once again the device which had proved so successful in the past, Dale and De Leeuw presented themselves as reincarnations of the Yalis' legendary ancestors Marik and Kugwarak. This the Yalis accepted, but a query arose over the five black members of the party. It was easily explained away. They, too, the missionaries assured them, were tribal ancestors, whose misfortune it had been to die upon the mountains and as a result no ritual burial had been given them, and this had prevented their reincarnation as whites.

The missionaries explained what was proposed while the Yalis listened in stunned silence. De Leeuw appears to have suffered a moment of self-questioning, evoking an appeal for divine guidance which Richardson faithfully quotes. '"Lord, you knew," Bruno prayed, "when you created this valley that this conflict of interest would arise. You could have provided a slope for the airstrip somewhere else ... since you didn't, this conflict of interests must be part of your plan. Perhaps you intended to work through it."'

The response must have been reassuring, for an immediate start was made in the demolition of houses and gardens. The village water-hole was filled in, and its sacred stones used to patch a wall. 'Stan, Bruno, and the five Danis,' Richardson writes, 'found the Yalis' stone-hewn boards to be of excellent quality and promptly used them to begin new and larger dwellings for their own need ...'

A down-payment had been offered in salt; final settlement in axes and cowrie shells was to be made after the gardens had been cleared away. For this work – to take some months – the labour of several hundred Yalis would be required, but suddenly the Yalis would have none of it, and withdrew in silence to watch while the missionaries pitched into the work which imported labour would have to finish.

And with this a too frequent imposture began to wear thin. The next year Dale and De Leeuw were intercepted in the act of measuring out another intended strip, and after attempting to frighten off the Yalis by bombarding them with thunderflashes, they were attacked and killed, and eaten. In reprisals undertaken with police co-operation several Yalis lost their lives. Total war in the valleys broke out when an epidemic of flu – previously unknown in Irian Jaya – was blamed by the tribespeople on the missionaries, and there were attempts to evict them from their stations.

Robert Mitton, an Australian geologist working in the area, describes some of these events in *The Lost World of Irian Jaya*. Once, when a missionary plane came under attack and the pilot took off with arrows hitting the plane, 'it then proceeded to dive-bomb the attackers while Kujit (the local missionary-in-chief) held them at bay with a shotgun. At the same time there was an attack at Anguruk which resulted in eight attackers being shot. It will be interesting to see what happens next.'

What, in fact, happened was the massacre at Nipson in May 1974. As Mitton puts it, 'the locals had had enough of the Good Word, burned down the missionary's house and ate his Biak preacher and twelve of his assistants. Fortunately for them the missionaries (including Kujit) were in the United States on leave.' Under subsequent interrogation, one of the attackers stressed that this cannibalistic spree had nothing to do with a taste for human flesh, being no more than the ultimate expression of vengeance.

In Baliem, sixteen years later, the atmosphere was one of genial and productive calm. This fifty-mile-long valley must offer an almost unique example of a Stone-Age people who, having tried what the West has to offer, has resolutely and happily turned away, re-immersing itself with evident relief in the timeless past. Whatever the attempts made to force the Danis to put on clothes, to become wage-earners and consumers living in hygienic villages, they have preferred a neolithic environment, continuing to live in the closest contact with the soil in hearty family groups occupying a vast amount of space, where there is no shortage of food, leisure and entertainment. About one-third of the 100,000 Danis are nominally Catholics, who go to church whenever they can to sing splendid hymns of local manufacture and enjoy contact with the invigorating seats. Once every five years the good fathers look in the other direction when the Danis pay their respects to Nompae, principal spirit ancestor, with spectacular feasting.

Ritual warfare remains the principal stumbling block to progress as defined by those insisting that ultimately in this world we should all be the same. These periodical blood-lettings, it has been suggested, are a by-product of too much leisure. But a more generally held opinion sees them as a carefully regulated solution to the problem of adjusting population to resources. Whatever their cause, the Danis have evolved in a climate of recurrent small-scale wars, and enforced abstention from such bellicosity produces withdrawal symptoms in the tribe, comparable to those of drug addiction in an individual.

Small, clandestine flare-ups occur occasionally, it is said, that are even promoted by tourists prepared to pay big money for spectacular photography. Real battles, too, in the theatrical style of the past, happen once in a while. I was able to find a young Dani, Namek, with a few words of English, who had taken part in one of these and was proud to have been wounded in the knee. He explained that a piece of uncultivable land had been set aside by two clans, purely to provide, as required, the pretext for battle. In the spring of 1990 when my friend, a clan member who had been living for fifteen years in another part of the country, had received what amounted to a call-up to defend the disputed territory against invasion, this, emotionally, he had been unable to resist. Hardly pausing to say goodbye to his family, he grabbed a spear and set off for the scene of action, determined to be in time for the ritual challenges and first discharge of arrows.

Normally in such conflicts combatants do their best to avoid killing each other by spearing their opponents in the rear when they turn to run. This time something went wrong and there were a number of deaths, involving both sides in costly reconciliation feasts and burdensome and protracted funeral rites. Namek took me to the place of battle, a barren hillside beside which, at that moment, two women passed in solemn perambulation. One appeared to be in her twenties, and as a sign of mourning her face and body were coated with dried yellow clay. Her brother, Namek said, had been killed in the battle, and she would remain in mourning for a year. The older woman, her constant companion, was required to ward off the evil spirits that fed on grief. In the old days, one or two of this girl's fingers would have been chopped off. The women had raised a great protest, he said, at the introduction of a law forbidding such amputations.

At Kulageima, Namek's present home, I met the 'big man' of the village, who had contributed handsomely to the dedication of a new church in the vicinity by the provision of a large number of pigs, each one to be dispatched by his son, a proficient archer, with a single arrow through the heart. He was a man infused with the dignity of power: a conservative with correctly blackened forehead, an ancient cowrie necklace, white cockatoo feathers curving down from behind ears cropped of their lobes in token of some old bereavement, and a penis gourd of modest length and without decoration. Despite the extreme restraint practised by Danis in sexual matters, the chief had twenty wives and forty-two children. His principal wife, smoking a cheroot, came into view, a pretty woman some thirty years his junior, who had dressed herself for the church fiesta in possibly the only T-shirt to be seen in the Baliem, bearing a vulgar inscription in French.

The background was full of bustle and laughter. The Danis spend much time tidying up their surroundings, and young girls were dashing about with bundles of fresh grass to be spread over the earthen floors of the houses, and renewing mats upon which feet had to be wiped at their entrance. In preparation for the fiesta they had painted their skin with patterns of coloured dots, and, by way of further decoration, white spectacle frames round their eyes. The chief gestured in their direction, shaking his head with a broad-minded smile. '*Weh, weh*,' he repeated over and over again. It was a formal welcome, which included an invitation to claim a vacant space on the floor of the men's hut in which a fire burned smokily to frustrate the mosquitoes, but was at least warm.

A few hundred miles to the east the Melanesians of Papua New Guinea, under an Australian-style government, had been hurled in a couple of generations into a recognisable version of the developing world, and there were depressing accounts in the guidebooks of hazards the traveller might be expected to encounter. 'In some areas rascals terrorise the community . . . many Papuans live in shanty towns, there is little work and drunkenness is rife . . . crime is the favourite topic of conversation . . . houses are barricaded – the middle class live in barbed-wire fortresses . . . you are vulnerable even in a group, so keep off the streets . . . risks of hold-ups are far greater at night.' It is an apocalyptic prospect, from which the eye turns with relief to a survival of other times.

1991

NAMEK'S SMOKED ANCESTOR

THE ONE THING that impressed me about the airport building at Wamena was an enormous artificial flower placed in the path of arriving passengers. This, a four-foot-across polystyrene Rafflesia, had been so painstakingly created that for a moment I thought I detected a sickly floral fragrance in its vicinity, whereas the fact was that the airport as a whole smelt of nothing but a powerful anti-mosquito spray in use. After the flower came the information desk, where I enquired for a taxi driver who, according to a Jayapura agent, could usually be found at the airport and was the only Dani in Wamena who spoke English reasonably well. I was taken to the back of the building, where he was pointed out to me, occupied with some tourists who were photographing him in national garb. He was short for a Dani, with glittering eyes and a black beard, and as he hurried forward at the end of the session to introduce himself, his limp translated itself into a skip. His flat fur hat, of the kind once worn by Henry Tudor, enhanced a dignity by no means impaired by his nakedness. Apart from this head covering, he wore nothing but a two-foot yellow penis gourd held in the upright position by a string round the waist. The scrotum had been tucked away at the base of the gourd, exposing the testicles in a neat, blueish sac. This did not surprise me, for as the plane taxied in I had noticed half a dozen naked men unloading a cargo plane.

We shook hands. Namek repeated the Dani greeting '*weh,weh*' (welcome) a number of times, excused himself, went off and came back wearing ill-fitting ex-army jungle fatigues. It now turned out that the taxi in which he had a quarter share was the magnificent ruin of an ancient Panhard-Levasseur, formerly owned by a Javanese Raja, which now awaited us, refulgent with polished brass, at the airport gate. In this we travelled in some state to a *losmen* (hotel) he recommended, where I took the austere room offered for one night, then, after a quick tidy-up, joined him in a species of porch, opening on to the street, where we discussed the possibilities of an investigatory trip into the interior.

By chance we had arrived in the midst of a minor crisis. The town had been showered overnight by large flying insects which, although harmless, were of menacing appearance. Many of them had found their way into the *losmen*, where they hurtled noisily across rooms and down passages, colliding with staff and guests, and then, their energy exhausted, were added to the piles into which they had been swept, until time could be found to clear them away. Namek took a gloomy view of this phenomenon, promising, he assured me, a change in the weather, which was likely to be for the worse.

'How do you come to speak English so well?' I asked him.

'My mother was killed in an accident and a Catholic

father adopted me,' he said. 'From him I am learning English and Dutch.' He spoke in a soft sing-song, eyes lowered, as if soothing a child, then looking up suddenly at the end of each sentence as if for assent.

'Now I am a registered guide,' he said, 'no other taxi has assurance. Also I work in my garden. Tomorrow I will bring you sweet potatoes.'

'Are you married?'

'I have two wives,' he said. 'My father had two handfuls. That is the way we say for ten. We are always counting on fingers.' He raised his eyes to mine with a quick, furtive smile. 'You see we are going downhill.'

'Catholic, are you?'

'In Wamena all Catholics.'

'Doesn't your priest object to the wives?'

'For Danis they are making special rules. It's okay for them to have many wives. I cannot catch up with my father. Times now changed. Maybe one day I will have one wife more. That is enough.'

There was a moment of distraction while the *losmen*'s cat raced through over the furniture in chase of the last of the fearsome insects. Namek showed me the agent's letter to him. 'My friend says you are wanting to see of our country. May I know of your plans?'

'I haven't any,' I said. 'This is just a quick trip to get the feeling of the place. What ought I to see? Merauke-Sorong? The Asmat, would you say?'

'You may show me your *surat jalan* [travel permit]. Did you put down these places?'

'I only put down the Baliem. Can the others be added here?'

'No. For that you must go back to Jayapura for permission to go to these places.'

'In Jakarta they said it could be done here.'

'They are wrong. Go to the police office and they will tell you.'

'It seems a waste of time. Let us suppose I go back – am I sure of getting the permissions?'

'Here nothing is sure. One day they are telling you yes, the next day they say no. They will not agree to tell you on telephone. Now also the telephone is not working.'

'So what do you suggest?'

He was reading the *surat jalan*, going over the words, letter by letter, with the tip of his forefinger, each word spoken softly, identified, and its meaning confirmed.

'With this *surat jalan* you may go to Karubaga,' he said.

'And what has Karubaga to offer?'

'Scenery very good. Also you are seeing different things. There are women in Karubaga turning themselves into bats.'

'That's promising,' I said. 'How do we get there?'

'By Merpati plane,' he said. 'To come back we are walking five days. In Karubaga you may find one porter. Maybe two. Also one bodyguard.'

'Why the bodyguard? Cannibals?'

The thick beard drew away from his lips as he humoured me with a smile. 'No cannibals. Sometimes unfriendly people.'

The many frustrations of travel on impulse had left their brandmark of caution on me. 'What are the snags?' I asked. 'Tell me the worst.'

'Very much climbing,' he said. 'Heart must be strong. *Surat* to be stamped by police in five villages. At Bakondini no river-bridge. Porters may bring you on their backs across, or rattan bridge to be built one day, two days – no more. Every day now it is raining a little.'

As he spoke a shadow fell across us. Part of the porch was of glass, and through it I saw that, where a patch of blue sky had shown only a few minutes before, black, muscled cloud masses had formed and were writhing and twisting like trapped animals. A single clap of thunder set off a cannonade of reverberations through the echoing clapboard of the town, morning became twilight, and then we heard the rain clattering towards us over the thousand tin roofs of Wamena. Pigs and dogs were sprinting down the street, chased by a frothing current, then disappearing behind a fence of water.

The rain stopped, the sun broke through, and the steam rose in ghostly, tattered shapes from all the walls and pavements of the town. Mountain shapes, sharp-edged and glittering, surfaced in the clear sky above the fog. 'In one hour all dry again,' Namek said.

We came back to the question of travel. 'I'll think about Karubaga,' I said. 'Any suggestions about using up the afternoon?'

'We may go to Dalima to visit my smoked ancestor,' Namek said. 'For this we may bring with us American cigarettes.'

In Wamena they smoked clove cigarettes, and there was a long search in the market for the prized American kind that were rarely offered for sale. By the time we found a few packets, the shallow floods had already dried away, and we set off. We chugged away on three cylinders into the mountains to the north, left the car sizzling and blowing steam at Uwosilimo, and trudged five miles up a path to Dalima. In these off-the-beaten-track places the Dani had held on to their customs until the last moment, cropping ears and amputating fingers years after such exaggerated expressions of bereavement following the deaths of close relatives had been stamped out elsewhere. Persons of great power and influence, known as *kain koks*, were not cremated in the usual way but smoked over a slow fire for several months and thereafter hung from the caves of their houses, where they continued to keep a benevolent eye on the community for decades, even centuries, until the newly arrived Indonesians launched their drive against 'barbarous practices', took down the offending cadavers and burned them or threw them into the river.

Namek's ancestor had been one of the few successfully hidden away, and now, in a slightly relaxed atmosphere, he could be discreetly produced for the admiration of visitors with access to cigarettes from the USA which, he let it be known through a shaman, was the offering he most appreciated.

The whole village turned out for us in holiday mood, the women topless and in their best grass skirts, and the men in the local style of penis gourds, with feathers dangling from their tips. We distributed cigarettes and the current *kain kok* tottered into view, overwhelmingly impressive with the boar's tusks curving from the hole in his septum, his bird-of-paradise plumes, and his valuable old shells. Beaming seraphically, he punched a small hole in the middle of the cigarette and began to smoke it at both ends. He was the possessor of four handfuls of wives, and of this Namek said in a sibilant aside, 'Now he is old, and his women play their games while they are working in the fields.'

With this the smoked ancestor was carried out, having

been crammed for this public appearance into a Victorian armchair. One arm was flung high into the air with a malacca cane grasped in the hand. The other hand, reaching surreptitiously down behind his back, held the polished skull of a bird. The Tudor-style hat affected by all the clan's leading males was tilted jauntily over an eye socket, and the ancestor's skin was quite black and frayed and split like the leather of an ancient sofa. His jaws had been wrenched wide apart by the fumigant, and now the old *kain kok* lit a Chesterfield, puffed on it, and wedged it between the two molar teeth that remained. Behind him descendants of lesser importance awaited their turn to make similar offerings to the ancestor.

The scene was in part grotesque but abounding in good cheer. The women rushed at us giggling and happy to show off their mutilated hands, and the men seemed proud of the tatters of skin which were all that remained of their ears. The village was a handsome one, scrupulously clean and well kept, and I was fascinated to see that the villagers had uprooted trees in the jungle and replanted them in such a way that they drooped trusses of fragrant yellow blossoms over the thatches of their houses. These attracted butterflies of sombre magnificence, which fed on the nectar until they became intoxicated and then toppled about the place like planes out of control, and were chased ineffectively both by the children and the village dog. In such Dani communities it is more or less share and share alike, and it seemed that in the allocation every child over the age of seven had been given a half-cigarette. These they were puffing at vigorously, and the village was full of the sound of their jubilation.

1993

GUATEMALA REVISITED

THIS WAS THE latest of five visits to Guatemala. The previous one was back in 1970 and had coincided with one of the country's frequent states of emergency. The plane landed at Aurora Airport only twenty minutes in advance of a rigorous curfew imposed at 9 p.m., and the taxi driver assured me that this would be taken so seriously that, if I failed to get to my hotel by that time, I should have to take refuge wherever I could. We made it with a minute to spare, the city lights went off and the guests in the Pan-American Hotel huddled for the rest of the evening under the feeble illumination supplied by a generator. During the night I was awakened by occasional shots, one of which smashed a window in the hotel's dining room. Next morning life had returned to the confused and bustling normality of any Central American capital.

The shots in the night turned out to be no more than a part of present excitements, for 25 November, the day after my arrival, had become by governmental decree the date on which Yuletide celebrations were to begin. Perhaps in an effort to redress the tensions of the moment, they were to be exceptionally prolonged, occupying a whole month, and on a scale never previously attempted. By nine in the morning I was down fighting my way through the crowd on Sixth Avenue for a view of the first of the parades. Here the city's leading stores had complied with the order to spray their windows with plastic snow, fireworks were popping off everywhere and through the sound of these explosions a hundred loudspeakers spread through this part of the city the tremendous nostalgia of Bing Crosby dreaming of a white Christmas. Santa Claus came into sight on a float, preceded by boys carrying cardboard cut-outs of reindeer and one brandishing a pair of cast-off antlers donated by the zoo. Father Christmas, in the moment of passing, had discovered a bottle of *aguardiente* in his robes, and opening a breach in the cottonwool stuck to his face, shoved the neck into his mouth and swallowed. He was drunk.

Next day I met Don Luis Aguilar, Governor of Guatemala City and Province, at the British Embassy party. He was the possessor of the slightly ferocious kind of good looks that the Indians much admired, and they were said to have used him as a model for the carved masks used in their dance-dramas, usually based on tragic themes. Aguilar was an Anglophile who had read history at King's and spoke English with a smooth Cambridge accent. When I told him that I lived fairly close to his Alma Mater, we were instantly joined in one of those shallow but vehement friendships based on a geographical accident. 'Anything I can do for you, dear boy. Any time. Just give me a ring.'

For a moment I took him seriously. I remembered an incident in a side-street a few yards from the rejoicings of the previous day. The police had used extreme violence in the arrest of a young man assumed by onlookers to be an urban guerrilla. Aguilar's offer seemed to suggest an opportunity to bolster the dramatic content of a piece I was writing for a London newspaper, and I asked if he could fix a meeting for me 'with one of your political prisoners'. Nothing changed in the smile of power that the Indians held in such esteem, as he twirled his glass. Although no fellow guests were in the vicinity, he lowered his voice. 'Sorry, dear boy, we have none. A luxury we can't possibly afford.'

This was his way of telling me of the half-hidden conflict between the nation's Indian peasantry, whose numbers had been increasing at an uncomfortable rate, and 'normal' Guatemalans. Until this, the population had been composed of three million of each, but now, despite their great poverty and their backwardness, the Indians were pushing ahead. He warned me of the existence of a secret war in which no prisoners were taken. 'Dear boy, there are simply too many of them, and there isn't enough land to go round. Make sure you read what the President has to say about it in today's *Prensa Libre*.' I did. President Arana announced that the army had liquidated the largest guerrilla movement in Latin America, adding the information that in doing so 7,000 civilians, i.e. Indians, had been killed. Despite the communiqué's confident tone, the President warned of a continuing struggle. 'We are virtually in a state of Civil War,' he said, 'for with the arrival on the scene of the urban guerrilla, the battle has been transferred to the city.' Nevertheless, he concluded on a note of optimism, inviting foreigners, whose recent experience of life in Guatemala might not have been entirely a happy one, to return and enjoy a future, he promised, of peace and plenty. 'We are on the brink of a national transformation,' he assured them. Guatemala, he reminded readers, had always been entitled the Land of Eternal Spring. 'Now we face a winter of struggle from which, due to our sacrifices, we shall emerge into a new springtime – that of the soul.'

Twenty-five years passed, and in January of last year I received a letter from a Guatemalan friend – a successful young author with whom I had corresponded for some time – suggesting that the moment had come for a further visit to his country. Many places long out of reach because of guerrilla warfare were now accessible. He could borrow a four-wheel-drive vehicle able to cope with all but the worst of the dirt roads across the mountains. A few guerrillas were still about in areas likely to be of interest to us, but they were far easier to deal with, he assured me, than the police, contenting themselves normally, if one ran into them, with a political lecture plus at most a request for a few dollars to help with funds. A newspaper cutting illustrated the kind of situation that could arise when, in this case, about 200 motorists had been held up by an armed group on the Inter-American Highway and compelled to listen for two and a half hours to its leader's persuasive but interminable speech.

It was a project with immense appeal and in February I took the plane to Guatemala City, joining Federico as soon as possible after arrival in the small mountain town of Chichicastenango. Here, despite decades of President Arana's accurately predicted war, I was delighted once again to watch Indian notables in the ceremonial Spanish attire of the sixteenth century performing their pagan rites on the steps to the Santo Tomás church.

My suggestion was a visit to the Ixchil Triangle under the Cuchumatanes Mountains in the north. Its attraction was two-fold. It had always been impossibly remote and it was this remoteness that fostered originality in its arts and preserved ancient customs that had vanished elsewhere in parts of the country reached by better roads. Whatever remained of the artistic impulses of the Mayas of old was to be found in places that were too far from the towns to be influenced by the demands of commerce. The weavers of Nebaj and Chajul could not travel to the markets to sell what they produced. Thus designs remained pure and spontaneous, reflecting in some way, too, the lifestyle of these isolated people.

We accordingly set out in a borrowed Toyota Land Cruiser heading northwards through Santa Cruz del Quiché in the direction of Sacapulas, shortly after which we would turn off onto the unsurfaced road over the Chuchamatanes leading into the Triangle. Once again Guatemala on a perfect springlike day appeared at its best. It is a country of extreme, often unearthly, beauty, lying in the shadows of thirty-two volcanoes, its towns rattled constantly by earthquakes like dice in a box, its villages peopled by a race who rarely smiled, but sometimes giggled in a foolish way as if embarrassed, as I thought then, in the presence of tragedy.

For an hour or two it was easy going in the familiar surroundings of villages of clustered adobe huts and little rectangles of cultivation high on the mountainsides, frequently so steep that the peasants who worked them hung on to ropes. Sometimes we passed an army patrol, their faces transformed with the sudden ugliness that comes when peasants are turned into soldiers, marching well spaced to avoid destruction by a single volley. Despite all the twisting of the wheel to keep on an even keel, the car bucked and rolled and once in a while a void appeared between its front wheels, into which it dropped lopsidedly with a crash before hauling itself out. Pyramided hills zigzagged away into the jagged sky-tracery of the high sierra. We crawled round the edge of the landslides left by the 1976 earthquake, then the village of Nebaj, a sprawl of greyish adobe huts, came into view.

Suddenly, life was there bubbling up again in the sallow light and narrow streets. Women with pink mountain cheeks, in the most brilliant of blue *huipils* (blouses) and skirts, marshalled tiny, wistful piglets and scuttling ducks. The weaving on their garments ran riot in colour and design. Surrealist horses with green faces and red eyes carried their foals, and on each foal perched a quetzal bird in all its colours, with the longest of tails. It was a sight wholly unexpected after the desolation that had struck the village fifteen years before, when it had been the headquarters of the EGP (Guerrilla Army of the Poor) and the army had exacted a terrible retribution. Nevertheless, the blaze of peasant colour for which Nebaj was famous had survived the human slaughter.

We found the villagers kind and hospitable. They fed us with eggs and black beans and sold me a splendid *huipil* and we spent a cold, dark night in a hut before setting off in the early morning.

Chajul, principal objective of the journey, is the most isolated of the three villages of Ixchil. Suddenly the landscape had changed under the blue Alpine light, for it was covered with grasslike moss over which boulders had been scattered, torn by earthquakes from the cliffs.

The topiary of the winds had carved trees into strange shapes, and stopping once to admire the austere enchantments of the scene, I raised a cloud of grey butterflies among the pines.

In the thirty-odd miles to Chajul we saw not a single human being, not a building of any kind, not an animal. It was accepted that of the 450–500 villages destroyed in the troubles, many had once existed in this area. This journey was through countryside rescued from every trace of human intrusion and then, suddenly, the great white church of Chajul appeared among the hills, although there were strenuous miles to be covered before the houses clustered beneath it came into sight.

They proved to be low, windowless and painted in strong shades of crimson, purple and blue. The church dominating this inanimate scene had been built, as so many old Guatemalan churches were, at the top of a flight of steps on an eminence, in order to attract worshippers of old by what was hoped would remind them of a Mayan pyramid. We left the car, climbed the steps and found ourselves in a vast crepuscular cavern-scented interior containing nothing but half a dozen dark and contorted saints, hung in cages from which they gesticulated despairingly, as if in hope of escape. A naïve, crudely painted picture, some ten feet in length, had been propped against the open door. This was of naked corpses disfigured with horrific wounds, although all the faces were devoid of expression. NO OLVIDAD NEUSTROS MARTIRES (REMEMBER OUR MARTYRS), the lettering said.

From the top of the church steps we looked out over the mist-layered forest to the black triangle of a mountain top across the Mexican frontier. Twenty-five thousand refugees had fled there to shelter either in camps or in the houses of Mexican peasants as poor as themselves, who had received them willingly and looked after them, in some cases for fifteen years. It was this panic-stricken exodus, perhaps, from which Chajul had never recovered, and it had left an aftermath here of silence and emptiness. The sensation for me was heightened by the savage colours of this place, painted on walls as if a backcloth for a tragic drama of the past, which indeed the history of this village was.

In 1979 the Guatemalan Army undertook a series of operations described as punishments in the districts of Ixchil, Ixcan and other areas in which guerrillas were in action. Peasants believed to have sheltered guerrillas or to have supported them in any way were rounded up, interrogated and, as generally alleged, tortured, and then put on display in some convenient village – in this case Chajul – where all the local inhabitants were assembled to watch the punishment inflicted.

What took place in September 1979 in Chajul has been described in chilling detail in Rigoberta Menchú's book, *An Indian Woman in Guatemala*. Despite the extreme horror of the account, no official denial has ever been made as to its veracity, and in the changed climate of Guatemala the book can now openly be offered for sale.

The news of what was to happen had been spread through a wide area, and on the day before the army's punishment was to be administered to the suspects held in custody, Rigoberta, her father and mother crossed the mountains, walking all night to reach Chajul. Rigoberta's sixteen-year-old brother was among those to be punished in the presence of several hundred Indians brought in from other areas. Chajul was surrounded for the occasion by 500 troops and among them were a squad of *Kaibils* – commandos entrusted with work of the kind envisaged.

The village square under the church had been chosen for the staging of the final scene, and it was announced that any inhabitant failing to attend would receive the same punishment. The prisoners were paraded before the assembled crowd and their clothing was cut from them to display the tortures they had suffered. Rigoberta says that, due to his maltreatment, she had difficulty in recognising her brother, although her mother was able to convince herself that he had smiled at her. With the officer's long lecture on the political niceties of the day at an end, the prisoners were led away to a level space among the bushes at the side of the church, and the village audience was forced under guard to watch the last episode of the drama. Petrol was poured over the victims and they were set alight. After the burning Rigoberta, still watching closely, records: 'The bodies kept twitching . . . they kept twitching about.'

At the back of the woods, women in scarlet *huipils* and skirts now slipped in and out of houses. 'Where are all the village menfolk?' I asked, remembering then that the question hardly called for an answer. Federico's reply was heedless of sinister overtones. 'Some of them are still in the woods,' he said. 'They've been there half their lives, but they're beginning to come out now.'

It was well over twenty years since I had seen anything of Guatemala City, apart from the surroundings of the airport, and now, having parted company with Federico for a day or two, I returned to it in the certain knowledge that great changes would have taken place.

After the Second World War, when I first got to know it, the city continued to live fairly comfortably in the past. Landowners of the old school had their boots polished four times a day, and might wear spurs, although they had never ridden a horse. Visitors could be shocked at the sight of an Indian porter staggering up a leafy avenue with a chest of drawers strapped to his back, because it was cheaper to move furniture in this way than to hire a wheeled vehicle. The barefoot Indian waitress at the Palace Hotel hoped to be tipped with a wrapped sweet. Guatemala City of old had some wonderful survivals, including the market of the *Zopilotes* (small vultures), which not only cleaned the place up but could be taught good-natured co-operation in games of chance, as friends who lived there discovered, by throwing edible scraps into an expectant huddle of them and betting on which bird would carry it off.

Apart from musicians playing marimbas on the street corners it was a quiet place in those times. Nowadays it had become an inferno of traffic, with crashed cars piled one on top of another at the roadside. A big M shining mistily through the smog not only provided faint illumination but reminded Guatemalans, who had lived until now almost exclusively on chicken and rice, that a new future with McDonald's had arrived.

Regretfully, however, I was to decide that my once-favourite colonial capital had become sinister and possibly cruel. The guidebook warned travellers to book their hotel well in advance. 'The city,' as it puts it, 'is not a pleasant place to wander about looking for a room at night.' There was talk in the paper of new-style kidnappings carried out by gangs of enterprising youths from El Salvador. These slipped across the border for a working weekend in Guatemala, conducting their operations rather as though applying a fast-food-restaurant approach to the abduction business. Likely prospects were snatched from the streets, held for the shortest possible time and released on payment of a quite small ransom – $500 being the average demand. Federico's family had been unfortunate in this respect, for his mother had been held captive for six months and released only when the family's resources were exhausted.

The old capital, Antigua, always regarded as the most relaxed place in the country, was only an hour away by taxi, so I decided to go there and spend a few days in surroundings renowned for their tranquillity. The hotel recommended was of unusual interest for it had been built at immense cost on the ruins of the Convent of Santo Domingo, destroyed in one of the earthquakes for which Antigua has earned a melancholy reputation. It was dark by the time I arrived, with the hotel full of shadows and the lighting in the cavernous reception area so faint that I found it difficult to read the paper I was given to sign. Rooms were reached at the end of long passages in which dark saints, salvaged from the ruins, waited as if in ambush in their niches. Overpowered by the atmosphere, the guests talked in lowered voices. The Santo Domingo, I learned, was about a half a mile from the town's centre but, enquiring of the direction to take, I was dissuaded from going in search of bright lights by a warning that it was better to be off the streets by eight, and it was now coming up to nine.

Next morning the doubts and misgivings of the previous night were dispelled by the brilliance of the day. More churches, monasteries and convents had been crammed into a relatively small area here than anywhere else in the Spanish colonial possessions, and, although many had been thrown down by the terrific earthquakes of 1717, 1751 and 1753, the shining façades of such buildings that had survived floated above the city. Antigua held a refulgence of a special kind, softened by shadows from balconies and eaves, and above all the vast misted shape of the volcano that formed a background to so much of the city.

It was a Sunday and I walked down to the Plaza where, as was to be expected on this day in any Latin American town of standing, most of the innocent pleasures of life were on display. The Indians had flocked in to sell their weaving, to watch the clowns, to allow conjurors to take plastic balls from nostrils and ears, to listen to the evangelist talking about hell, and to squat in family circles in the gardens, keeping their innumerable children amused. Above all this place resounded with music of an exciting, even violent kind. For the first time I realised that the insistent, shrilling pipe-music of the mountain tops, everywhere in South America, also exists in Guatemala. A group of youngsters who might have been coming here from among the llamas of the altiplano of Bolivia were in frenzied action with panpipes and flutes, over the hugely amplified percussion of a marimba through speakers fixed up on the wall of the neighbouring police station.

The quietest attraction of this day, and out of hearing of these excitements, was a solemn pilgrimage just around the corner to the shrine of Hermano Pedro in the Franciscan church where stickers, in gratitude for his most recent miracles of the hundred or so performed annually, are stuck all over the walls. Among new additions were thanks to the saint for saving the driver of a car from death after a wheel had fallen off, and for a widow's vision of her husband in paradise, noting in her little tribute that some rejuvenation in his appearance had taken place after death.

I amused myself in and around the Plaza until about 6.30 p.m. when, with the day darkening, the music came to an end. Now the clowns wiped the paint from their faces and packed up their gear. In half an hour it would be dark. The streets were beginning to empty and Indian family groups had already curled up in neat ancestral fashion under the arcades where the foreign backpackers sprawled among them. I wondered how many Indians were enjoying the experience. A friend who spoke fluent Maya-Quiché and had employed an Indian couple to look after him had heard them refer to their employers as the male, or female, ghosts. I learned from him that some Indians sincerely believed whites to be malevolent spirits, in whose power Indians found themselves temporarily entrapped.

Accustomed to the scene in the social centre of other Latin American towns, where the joys and sorrows of life are prolonged almost indefinitely after dark, I was a little disquieted by this abrupt ending to the day, and it was with reluctance that I took one of the last taxis back to the Santo Domingo.

The next day I was told that the best hope of more cheerful lodging was to be found in the Calle de la Concepción. This was almost a foreign colony in a single street, with European-style restaurants that stayed open until ten, including an Italian one run by a Neapolitan who offered to sing to his customers on Saturday evenings. There were as well several promising guesthouses, but all were taken over by Americans who had come down for the winter. The American proprietress of one rang a friend and found me a room. It was hardly any distance further from the centre than the Calle de la Concepción, she assured me. Why should this be of importance? I asked, and she told me that Concepción might be a little better in the matter of security. Two or three armed robberies happened daily in Antigua, according to the newspaper, she said, and a Spanish student had been stabbed only a few days before. 'This is really a little town within a town,' she said, 'and we aim to keep it that way.'

The house she thought I would like was on a street of fine old buildings, with little passing traffic and a minimum of street lights. It turned out to be rather grand. Servants came and went softly, branches loaded with exotic blooms drooped over the pavement of a vast courtyard, and there was an inspiring view of the tip of the volcano over a wall. It turned out that apart from the staff I was the only occupant. The police station was only a stone's throw away in the direction of the Plaza, but there was no comfort in its proximity, for the English-language newspaper, the *Guatemala Weekly*, reported that an armed robbery had taken place *outside* it only a few days before.

The high spot of previous stays in Guatemala had always been the ritual excursion to Lake Atitlán, for a day or two to be spent in one or other of the twelve villages on its shores, where the cones of so many volcanoes, skirted with black forests, seemed almost to duplicate the enchantments of South-East Asia. Writing of it back in the Thirties, Aldous Huxley had described himself as almost surfeited by its beauty, and coming down from the highlands when the shining contours of water under the volcanoes first came in sight, the hope was that this beauty had survived. It was not to be fulfilled. Huxley, in those days, might have watched a palisade of white cranes up to a mile in length wading in the lake's margin, while others, awaiting their turn to descend on the fish, made languid patterns of movement in the sky. Since then Atitlán had suffered from the vandalism of war and of tourist development, and now the great birds, and most other forms of wildlife, stayed away.

So I took the ferry to Santiago where, under misted volcanoes, the beauty of Atitlán returned. Santiago had managed in some way to resist the influences that had despoiled other lakeside villages. Perhaps there was something in the character of its people, who were Tzutuhils and notable for their pugnacity and independence, that made this possible. Whereas the Cakchiquels had shown little resistance to the Spanish invaders, the Tzutuhils put up a fight.

Above all, these people resist change and are defenders of the status quo, and bearing this in mind, it surprised me to discover that two Protestant evangelist missions had opened up, entering not only into vigorous competition with each other for souls but with the easy-going and somewhat Indianised Catholicism of the Church of Guatemala. It was at the end of the Second World War that the first of the evangelists arrived, and one of these launched a campaign to outlaw garments which, as he believed, were woven with pagan designs. He caused frustration among collectors, particularly foreign visitors, by paying above market prices for items with suspect weaving, which – although sometimes valuable antiques – went straight onto the bonfire. In the end the Council decided he was damaging the tourist business, and he was sent on his way. Nowadays, I learned, the evangelists no longer ordered members of their flock to dress like 'normal' Guatemalans, but at most suggested that they might suffer from a loss of status by the use of 'old-fashioned' modes of dress and, if employed, could expect to be paid lower wages.

By good luck an Indian wedding was being celebrated at the smaller mission at the time of my arrival. It was a highly Westernised affair. An old car with a sticker on the windscreen saying, CRISTO TE AMO was parked at the front entrance, and I snatched a glance through the window at the tiny brown triangle of the bride's face through her veil. Revivalist music burst out of the door we had reached at the back, and I had a view of tight-jacketed Indians, some in black, at the moment when the hymn ended and the pastor signalled for clapping.

The music, played on a variety of unfamiliar instruments, now changed to an Indianised version of *The Wedding March* and the small bride and her groom were about to enter the building by the further door. It may have been that in clambering down from the car, her Western-style wedding dress had become disarranged, for in the instant before she passed out of sight there was a glimpse of skirt beneath, and the dramatic purple and white of the Indian style of Santiago. I was relieved. There had been a change, but at least the Indians here were still far from a transformation from proud Tzutuhils into poor whites.

In Atitlán I was mercifully out of touch with newspapers for a few days, but arrived back in Antigua to coincide with a spate of journalistic gloom. At the end of the years of military dictatorship the time was at an end when eight leading journalists could be murdered for revealing to their readers too much of what went on behind the scenes. Now at last the press was free and the awful secrets tumbled from a Pandora's box in which, at the end, only hope remained.

Now it was safe for the mass graves of the resistance to be opened. While I was away, one had been found in a children's playground, out of bounds for years, from which it was estimated that 200 corpses would be recovered. In nearby Uspantan the remains of ninety persons who had fallen under suspicion had been disinterred in a single week. *La Prensa Libre* listed seven villages where the bones of a thousand dissidents might still be hidden away.

With a decline in the statistics of current murders, the police corruption capturing the headlines was of an order never experienced before. *Guatemala Weekly* reported instances of police officers robbing pedestrians in Guatemala City, and gave details of a system of daily quotas paid by patrolmen to their superiors as a portion of their income from corruption. Criminals sent to jail, the report alleged, could buy their way out and be back in action in a few days. It was a situation in which vigilante justice was everywhere on the increase. In Patzún, householders took habitual robbers from police custody and beat them to death. The residents argued that in the past such men had always been able to pay for their freedom.

Some newspapers still seemed a little nervous at drawing attention to the misdemeanours of persons in high places. Others, such as *Siglo XXI*, trod resolutely on thin ice. It published, for example, full details of the strange case of Colonel Cruz Mendez, Commander of the Aurora International Airport in Guatemala City and a gang of car thieves. These had driven off in a brand-new and highly desirable Mitsubishi belonging to an influential foreigner, who carried enough weight for the three squad cars to be dispatched in chase. Their headlong pursuit led to Colonel Mendez's house, where the thieves took refuge. The police were refused entry, and the Colonel's lawyer, appearing on the scene, told them they must leave unless they could produce a judicial order. This could not be obtained. Although Colonel Mendez received the powerful support of the Minister of Defence, his explanation that what had happened was 'the result of a simple confusion' was hard to accept and he was suspended from duty.

There was a glut of sensational news items that week. Indian peasants who had clearly not yet learned their lesson had invaded eighteen estates. What were described as 'official' bands of criminals were under investigation by the military, and kidnappers had abducted a party of girls from a school bus. Yet among all this drama and violence a single incident, which in earlier times would have been considered a minor offence, resisted all efforts to dismiss it from the front page. This was the case of the President and the milkman.

On the first Sunday of the month of February, the newly elected President Alvaro Arzú was riding with his wife and a party of army officer friends in a country lane on the outskirts of Antigua when a Suzuki pickup driven by twenty-four-year-old Sas Rompich came charging out of a side road and ran over a rider and horse before charging at the President. According to the Ministry of the Interior's report, the attack was foiled by an escort car racing forward to place itself between the President and his assailant, and blocking the assailant's escape. With this, a Captain Lima, throwing himself from his horse, wrenched open the door of Rompich's car, caught him by the throat and shot him three times. It can be taken for granted that, apart from accepting the news of Rompich's death, nobody in Guatemala believed this account.

However, whereas according to experience the story should have been dropped by the press after a couple of days, for once this did not happen. Few eyebrows of old would have been raised over an obvious fiction, but in the new era of openness things were different and disbelief had slipped in through the back door.

For the fact was that Rompich turned out to be no obvious assassin, but a milkman out on his rounds with a car laden with milk bottles, until it was his huge misfortune to encounter the President's cortège. Newspapermen were told by the family that he might have had a drop too much to drink at the time, and once in a while was drunk for two days or so. At worst, then, this might have been a case of dangerous driving. No horse or rider had been run over or damaged in any way. The newspapermen now referred ironically to 'a pseudo-*attentat*', or 'the supposed attack', and whatever hope there might have been in some quarters that public interest might now subside vanished with the publication of the Attorney General's charge that material evidence had disappeared. This included sabre scabbards found near Rompich's car, provoking sinister rumours of sword-play as well as proven gunfire. A further report from the Attorney General's office was that Rompich's shirt, with possible evidence of wounds other than those produced by Captain Lima's bullets, had been spirited away. Next the public was to learn that the victim's family had received mysterious warnings to keep their mouths shut 'or else . . .'. It seemed to some Guatemalans that the bad old days had returned.

Rompich's end had been defined in vague Guatemalan law as an 'extra-judicial execution', of which there had been a multitude in the country's recent history, but perhaps his essentially gentle profession, in contrast with the extreme violence of his ending, touched a nerve of sympathy in the nation's breast. Suddenly he was referred to not by name, but with a kind of affection as *El Lecherito* – the little milkman. Writing in *La Prensa Libre*, the distinguished journalist Fernando Molino said, 'It is important that this episode should provide the government with the opportunity to defend what we see as right. If not, and what has happened is to be settled in the way things have so often been in the past, we shall be forced to abandon all hope of change, and put aside faith in a just future.'

It was a viewpoint exactly reflecting the feelings of most Guatemalans in the street.

1997

AFTER THE MOON-WALK

THE *Observer* SENT me to Honduras, which, barring Haiti, the poorest country in the Western Hemisphere, and where I talked to a young man on a banana plantation who told me he hadn't eaten meat since fed with it by his mother as a sickly child. Although poor, I found the Hondurans extremely devout, Tegucigalpa being the only capital city I have ever seen where traffic snarl-ups were caused not by normal traffic but by head-on encounters by competing religious processions in the narrow streets. Most foreigners preferred to stay by the sea down at La Ceiba in the picturesque tropics, where there were humming birds pinned by the beak into every flower, soft light romanticised the hulks of decayed planes at the edge of the airfield, and the Picaroon Hotel recommended six-ounce steaks and Black and White whisky mixed with Coca-Cola.

All journalists in Tegucigalpa were expected to present themselves to the President, General Paz, and in due course I called at the palace, a modest building by Latin American standards flanked by shops selling handbags and scuba-diving equipment in the main street of the town. International interest had been aroused by a covert war conducted by 'Contras' under Honduras's protection against the country's recently-turned-socialist neighbour, Nicaragua. The hope was that a way could be found to persuade the General to come out into the open about his intentions, and I had been given advice as to the best way of tackling him by one of our diplomats who had been posted here for a short while. Despite the rough-and-ready methods attributed to most Latin American dictators, he said, Paz was milder than most and, passing on what was evidently a valuable tip, he told me that the General collected stamps, in particular commemorative issues. Bearing this in mind I put in a few hours' study of the subject before setting out on this trip.

I was seen at the palace by an exceptionally pleasant young aide, who spoke English well and lost no time in telling me that he expected to visit our country in the near future. The President, he said, was out of town but was expected back any day. There would be no difficulty in arranging an interview, he thought, but as the General's movements were unpredictable he suggested that I call early next morning, and should there be no news of His Excellency, perhaps again on the morning after that. The photographer Alain Le Gazemeur had been with me throughout this Central American journey and now there was an urgent *sotto voce* interruption from him, asking if a photograph would be permissible. 'Absolutely,' the aide said. 'The General is very well disposed towards the British people. He will be happy to be photographed.'

Alain had already mentioned an ambition to photograph a real live dictator turned out in the full-scale, ridiculously pompous style they often assumed. Would the General consent to don dress uniform for the occasion? he wanted to know, and the aide, smiling as encouragingly as ever, said he was sure he would.

'All medals and eyeshades?' Le Gazemeur asked.

'Whatever you wish,' the aide said. 'His Excellency is accustomed to co-operate with the press.'

It was arranged that we be at the palace at 8 a.m. next day. This we did, to be told by our friend that the General's return had been delayed. We presented ourselves on the morrow at the same time and for two days in succession after that, but of the General there was no further news.

The President's aide's name was Arturo; about now our friendship had reached a point when he asked to be called Arthur, and he placed a forefinger to his lips and took me aside.

'You can keep a secret – that I am sure?' he said.

'Well, I certainly hope so.'

'I think I must tell you now. The General has not been away from Tegucigalpa. He is here, but he has been in a drunken condition for one week.'

'I see, but that's a pity. So we've been wasting our time.'

'Tomorrow it is certain you may see him. He is to be present at a dinner given by Christian Businessmen for Colonel James Irwin. You have heard of him?'

'Didn't he walk on the moon?'

'He was the eighth man. Now he is touring the world as a Christian missionary, and the General has announced he will choose this day to accept Christ by becoming a Southern Baptist. He will be at the dinner, and you and Mr Le Gazemeur are invited.'

The morrow came, and 6 p.m. on the dot saw the arrival of the Christian Businessmen, who discharged from the buses that had brought them from the airport, swept like a tidal wave of humanity into the vast, bare banqueting hall, and after a moment of genial confusion over place names began to settle themselves at the long tables. The Businessmen were very large and affable, discharging smiles as if under compulsion in all directions, and giving the impression of being unaware of the presence of the comparatively tiny and insignificant members of the hotel staff scampering to proffer their services.

Seated and settled eventually in a wide, hollow square, the guests were confronted by a long platform. Upon this at one end two empty chairs had been placed side by side, and at the other end General Paz occupied something that was not quite a throne. I heard, or imagined I heard, Le Gazemeur's sigh, for far from the promised dress uniform with its rows of medals, the General wore a blue suit with a white shirt and striped tie and was of markedly Indian appearance, with a neatly trimmed moustache and an unimpressive chin. His eyes were closed and my guess was that he was asleep. Beneath the platform two small soldiers, both possessing an extraordinary resemblance to the President, stood facing the diners, tommy-guns held in the present-arms position.

The midget Hondurans now reappeared with trolleys of food. Steak is rarely banished from Central American menus, and here it was once again, overlooked on each tray by four leading varieties of soft drinks. Until this moment there had been no sign of the astronaut and, as plates emptied, conversation based largely on religious and financial topics swelled almost to an uproar. Several more small tommy-gunners had drifted into sight and distributed themselves strategically round the room and I realised with a touch of alarm that Le Gazemeur had slipped away and was moving in a stealthy fashion in the direction of the General, a camera with its enormous lens at the ready. No attempt was made by the General's bodyguards to intercept him and, reaching the edge of the platform, he squatted down and raised the camera to his eye. General Paz's posture remained unchanged, his head bowed and motionless over a tray placed before him and held in some way on his knees. Alain later assured me that the General had been asleep, obliging him to shout almost in the presidential ear before he opened his eyes.

The General's return to consciousness coincided with the appearance of Colonel Irwin, bounding suddenly from behind a screen at the back of the stage to reach the first of the awaiting chairs. An outburst of clapping was abruptly cut off, to be followed by something like a mass murmuring produced by many throats, invented, as we were later told, by this religious association as an expression of approval and encouragement. Colonel Irwin raised an arm, the murmurs died away and, speaking in a powerful, high-pitched voice, he told his audience how honoured and glad he was to be with them. He had come to Tegucigalpa as leader of the High Flyer Foundation Christian Ministry, whose aims for worldwide conversion were fully described in a personally signed document that each one of those present would receive.

The Christian Businessmen were accompanied on this trip by an American acting as required both as interpreter and steward, and now as the Colonel took his seat this man stood, to explain that it was time for those wishing to solicit both the Colonel's blessing and advice to rise to their feet and do so. The steward had a prepared list of names, and he signalled to the man at its head, who stood and began a description of his problem.

It was a financial one, but there was an obligatory flavouring of religion not to be avoided in this context. A vocabulary based on market reports had been infiltrated with pious themes and the occasional mention of God's name. The Colonel, it seemed, was no financial illiterate and showed no disapproval of wealth gained, for example, by insider-dealing. A Christian Businessman had run into trouble with his income tax and the Colonel chastened him not unsympathetically with the biblical ruling 'Render unto Caesar the things that are Caesar's.' Another questioner clearly in search of market tips was told that oils were strong and likely to get stronger. Then, raising a declamatory hand to his audience in general, the Colonel asked them: what did a man require to become a successful investor? 'I'm a beginner in the market, so what do I do? Read all the financial columns, then stick my neck out? No, sir. I turn in prayer to the Lord for the vision that only he can give. Only then do I know I am ready to face the market.'

Colonel Irwin took his seat to a strong rumble of applause.

The questioning was now at an end. Alain was still manoeuvring for a better shot of the General, who had momentarily opened his eyes but only to settle in a more comfortable position. Colonel Irwin had taken his seat again and the chair vacant until this moment was now occupied by a Christian Businessman, who along with several other applicants had been able to book a brief counselling session with him. Moments later I was surprised at the approach of the steward with Arthur at his heels to inform me that, as a guest of the General, I was among those to be favoured in this way. 'You're next,' he said. 'You have five minutes, and remember no reference is to be made to the postal covers.' This was an illusion to the scandal about the 400 envelopes, imprinted 2 August 1971, taken without permission aboard *Apollo 15* and, as the Colonel had admitted in his autobiography, cancelled 'with our own cancellation device which worked in a vacuum' and sold to a German dealer. The proceeds, Irwin had stated in mitigation, were to be devoted to 'our children's education'. It was a mistake that overshadowed his subsequent career and it may have been this crisis that convinced him to devote the rest of his life to his mission.

At close quarters the Colonel seemed to possess the good looks of a mature film actor, with a muscular physique and small eyes narrowed as if in scrutiny of some not necessarily acceptable object. His manner, however, was genial. I received a hard handshake accompanied by what might have passed in mission circles as no more than a routine politeness – the question, 'Are you saved?' Just out of earshot the steward stood, his eye on his watch. So I was really to be allowed no more than five minutes to know anything more than the newspapers had said of this man's huge adventure. His book, *To Rule the Night*, does little more than sketch this in against a background of the commonplaces of an average life and the humdrum religiosity with which the author attempts to advance his beliefs. From this there are rare escapes, as in that tremendous moment when on its re-entry the spacecraft is 42,587 miles from the earth, appearing as a thin illuminated sliver in the black sky.

Irwin denied in our talk that he had experienced loneliness at any time during the flight. 'I entered into consciousness of the Lord's presence.' Smilingly he went on to describe God as his Mission Director. It was a designation he had used in the book he had written when he was grounded after a heart attack. 'It was God taking charge again,' he wrote. 'My Mission Director was changing my flight plan.'

Time, I realised, was almost up. Just below us more steak was being rushed to the Christian Businessmen. The President's head had fallen on his chest and, arm thrust up, the steward tapped urgently on his watch. We rose to our feet, and Irwin took my hand in a crushing grip. His wide smile was pleasant and reassuring. 'The Lord can be your Mission Director, too,' he said. 'Why don't you just call on him?'

1997